TOKYO LEGENDS
# All the World
# We Never See

**By David Keuning**

# TOKYO LEGENDS

# DEDICATION

To Anika, your warrior spirit inspires me.
And to Kai, you model the well-considered life.

# ALL THE WORLD WE NEVER SEE

## Contents

# ACKNOWLEDGMENTS

The efforts of several friends helped me bring this project to fruition:  Katie Chang who with a few simple words gave me encouragement early on in the writing process, Nathalie Razo who reminded me that I don't know everything, Valerie Coryell who did not allow a broken thumb to slow her comments and suggestions, and Leighanna Reichenbach who graciously proofed my work.

Chapter One
A Visit to Meiji Shrine

Years later when I had finally completed my samurai training, I would look back on this day and remember the moment we set out for the shrine. I didn't know it then, but it was to be my last moment as a normal kid. This was to be the last day that I would wake up normally, eat a normal breakfast (cereal) and leave the house believing the world was pretty much the same safe place I had always thought it was. My illusions about the world we live in were about to be shattered, but as I sat at the breakfast table talking with my brother and eating my cornflakes, I had no idea that my understanding of everything was about to come to a screeching halt.

A lot of adults you talk to will suggest that the world is a big and scary place – that it is full of danger and you have to watch out. Those same adults will say that kids somehow don't know what the world is really like. That you, if you are a kid, don't really see what you should. They like to hint that someday you will understand everything the way they do. Someday your understanding will improve. They say things like, "When you are my age you will understand..." as if they have a clear understanding of the world themselves: the good, the bad and the things in this world to be afraid of.

But believe me, those adults have no idea what they are talking about. Most of them are going through their lives with blinders on. The danger they are talking about is nothing at all. Just simple things of no real consequence. They have no idea what kind of real danger lies all around them – right beneath their feet. Real danger.  As in 'suck-out-the-marrow-and-grind-your-bones-to-dust' kind of danger.  These adults live their lives going to Starbucks and taking money out of their ATMs, never knowing the truth about the world around them.  They've got no idea. Listen. I know all about danger.

Don't get me wrong.  Before all this happened to me, I wasn't any different.  I was not some sort of special 15-year-old with super skills.  I was as wrapped up in that world as the rest of them.  My life was all about going to school and struggling to get my homework done.  Not a day went by that I didn't wish I had more friends.  I was only concerned with the things right in front of my eyes. I never thought about much outside of my normal routine. But as I said, that world was about to end for my brother and me. And the day that I am going to tell you about is the day that everything changed.

Even now I can see it in my mind's eye:  the wooden dining room table in our little house in Tokyo, the red carpet beneath the table – still pristine and not yet damaged/degraded/demoralized from years of wear and tear.  Myself at 15, awkward and emotional. (Somehow in my imagination I know I must "look" awkward although I'm not sure how.) My brown hair would still be short, cut just below my shoulders the way I had always worn it, not yet grown into the neat ponytail that I wear now as samurai.  My brother Ken sits next to me.  He could have been my clone – a younger, boy version of me with the same butter-toast skin and green-flecked eyes.  He would have been 12 at the time, annoying me with small talk and shoveling cornflakes into his mouth. My father would have been wearing one of his perfectly pressed shirts, eating with us before heading to the office – even though it was the weekend.

It was four days before Christmas, as I remember.  Of course, our conversation focused on our upcoming holiday plans. My father wanted to plan a party, but my mind had wandered away from the conversation at the breakfast table.

"Well, why not invite your friends too?" he was saying in defense of his Christmas party suggestion.  I knew what he wanted. His idea was to have some sort of picturesque gathering at our house. He saw visions of eggnog, mistletoe and songs around the fireplace.  For his part, he would invite a handful of business colleagues.  Any plan that started as a family activity with my father quickly became a business venture.  Oh, we had a place in it

2

too. In his plan, we would invite a bunch of our friends – better if they were rosy-cheeked, wholesome-looking and wore some attractive holiday fashions. He would want us looking like a well-dressed Old Navy commercial. We would do our part to sing a carol or two around the tree and then disappear so he could conclude some business. That's how it always was with my dad.

"You don't understand, Dad," I shot back. "All of our friends are going home to the U.S. or abroad for a vacation. We're the only ones who are going to be left in Tokyo."

"Yeah," Ken confirmed. "Not that she has any friends to invite," he slipped in.

I shot him my meanest glance and mouthed the word "Evil" at him, but he ignored it and kept explaining.

"Everyone in my class is going someplace cool. Bali, Phuket, Saigon. Or back to the States. You name it. Anywhere but here."

It didn't help that we went to an "international" school. To me it seemed like they picked all the misfits and losers from all over the world and dropped them together at a school in Japan. The classes were taught in English – to my great relief! – and we followed more or less the same patterns of school that we had always known. This was, in fact, our second time to live in Japan. My brother and I had both been born here. That was during my Dad's first rotation to the Tokyo office, but Ken remembered nothing of it and I remembered very little. Just bits and pieces. Back when we had a mom.

You'd think that the second time around would be a little easier for us. Having moved to Tokyo from California over the summer, we were the "new students" and it was only the end of our first semester. Even though I hated to admit it, my brother was right: despite my best efforts I had very few friends at school.

It's not as if I wasn't trying. We'd moved so much I felt like I knew the drill. My dad's job with the bank and his perpetual pursuit of advancement at the office meant that he was often on new assignments in new locales. For us, that meant we were always the new kids. New city. New house. New school. With enough practice you get good at that kind of thing.

It's just that I would get nervous around new people. I really wanted to make a good impression. I really wanted people to like me, but I'd say things so fast and people would take it the wrong way.

"That's not what I meant," I'd say, but it would be too late. I'd get so excited that my words would come out all wrong. I tried really hard to get people to like me, but my words would have the opposite effect. Note to self: not an effective strategy for making new friends.

The other kids at school weren't mean to us, just indifferent. We were the new kids and most of them never bothered to learn our names. To make matters worse, our teachers gave us an awkward welcome.

On my first day at school Mrs. Stephens, my homeroom teacher, stood me up in front of the class and struggled to say something good about me. She shuffled her notes trying to locate whatever sentence she had scribbled down but was unable to find it. She kept me in front of the class for what felt like an eternity and finally ended with, "And I'm sure we'd all like to welcome her."

There was weak clapping from a disinterested homeroom. Fortunately, the bell rang and saved all of us from more discomfort. I tried to give my best "ohmigosh-you-all-seem-so-wonderful" smile and went back to my desk to unpack my stuff. Needless to say, a semester hadn't changed much, and I was still lacking friends.

"We don't have anything to do here," I grumbled to my dad at the breakfast table, staring at my soggy cornflakes. My timing was off. I'd missed my window of opportunity to eat them and found only mush in my bowl. I complained to him, but I knew he would not tear himself away from his work to do anything for us.

He sighed.

"I guess you'll just have to make your own entertainment."

He loved to say that. As if we were going to sit around and play family games or something. I didn't bother to roll my eyes. Even if he ever stayed home, that wasn't going to happen.

For me at least, there was one glimmer of hope: the Winter Jam. If my father was obsessed with his quasi-business dinner/Christmas party, all I could think about was the Winter Jam. Planned for the last day of school before break, The Winter Jam was going to be great. It wasn't a competition, just a performance. No winners or losers. It was a bit like open mic night on the football field. I had wanted to find someone to play in a band with me. I didn't bother to ask the cool kids because I figured they would turn me down. I wasn't brave enough to ask. After some struggle, I had finally worked up the courage to ask

Steph, the girl who sat next to me in math. She said no, she didn't play. Do you sing? I had asked. No, she didn't do that either. "Oh. Ha ha. Me either. Well, a little. Well, not much really. Okay then," I said waving goodbye.

Even now I tend to talk with my hands. My dad used to say if you tied my hands together I wouldn't be able to speak. I used to tell my friends it was because of my Italian upbringing. (It was a lie. I'm not Italian. I've never even been to Italy, but you know what I mean.)

Then I asked Morgan, from science class who had been nice to me during a science lab when I didn't know what I was supposed to be doing and had bumped a beaker that had shattered when it hit the floor. She said she was already in a group with two other girls. I could not bring myself to ask to be in the group with them. And Morgan never offered.

Not having any success with my peers, I had asked Ken and he agreed. Ken was becoming pretty good with the drums. He could definitely hold his own. He wouldn't embarrass me, and if I changed my mind and chickened out altogether, Ken wouldn't give me a hard time about it. In my imagination, the two of us would take the stage at Winter Jam, rock out a few great songs, and that would be my entrée into making a few friends at school. The cool kids would hear my guitar licks and want to be my friend. It was my version of the Prom Fantasy. You know the one where you buy a great dress and go to prom and all the other kids see you and everyone is like, "Who is that? She looks beautiful!" And then the cutest guy comes over and asks you to dance. And then you have a lot of friends.

While I was daydreaming this way, my elbow got in the way and a spoon clattered to the floor, discharging a payload of cereal and compromising the red carpet. Oops. Dad handed me a paper towel without comment.

"Look, it will be fun," he said, still lobbying for his party plan with executive intensity.

I pushed away from the table.

"Where are you going?" he asked, interrupted.

"It doesn't look like we are going anywhere," I spit out with more venom than I intended but then added, "I have some shopping to do. Ken, do I have to babysit you too?"

"Yeah, sure I will go with you," he said as though I had invited him to go along. I was secretly glad that he was coming. I wanted the company.

Looking back, I realize it was typical family small talk. Nothing out of the ordinary. The same conversation repeated more or less the same way at a thousand breakfast tables around the world. There was nothing to indicate that for our family this would be the last moment of normal.

In the many years since, as I have struggled through my samurai training, I have meditated on that moment at the breakfast table. What would have happened if I had stayed home? Would all my troubles have started? Or would I just be a normal kid living a normal life?

I wonder if there is a moment of great decision in every life – a pivot point that defines that life. You step to the edge of the cliff, but you don't always look over the edge. Sometimes you are worried about your nails or your shoe because it's untied. Perhaps you never notice that you are on the edge of a great precipice. If you notice that moment does it change the outcome? What would have happened if I had not left the breakfast table? If I'd never left the house? For me I didn't know that my life was about to change. I was thinking about other things. Mundane things. I certainly wasn't thinking about the extreme danger I was about to face. I didn't realize that this was the pivotal moment of my life.

"You wanna take the bus?" my brother asked me as we wandered downstairs, slipped our shoes on and pushed out the door.

I looked at him wanting to stay mad but for some reason my mood softened a bit. "Nah, it is a nice day. Let's take the shortcut through the shrine."

"Want to take Emvee?" Ken asked. Emvee was our Shiba ken, our Japanese dog. He had been with us for a couple of months. He had a wolf-like appearance with pricked ears, a foxy face and a thick coat. I read online that Shibas were closely related to wolves, more so than some other breeds of dogs. Our dog Emvee reminded me of what it must have been like for the people who domesticated wolves in the first place. We had found him chained to our mailbox with a note that said, "Present. From a friend of Yu."

I thought it was from someone with bad grammar who could not spell "you". We didn't have any friends in the neighborhood that I could think of. And who would give someone a dog as a present anyway? It remained a mystery but then my brother suddenly remembered that when my mom was with us, Dad had always called her "Yu". It was a little too weird to think that anyone would know our mom.   And again, why give someone a dog?

Looking at the note that we had kept and stuck on the refrigerator door, Ken mused, "Maybe his name is actually 'Present'? Here, Present.  Here, boy!"  We called him that for a while.  But the name never really stuck.

"Lousy name for a dog," my dad would say.

"I'm calling him 'M.V.'" I said.

"What's Emvee?" my brother asked.

"It stands for 'Mysterious Visitor'," I explain.

It turned out it didn't really matter what we called him, since he would never come to us anyway.  It wasn't as if he was deaf.  He obviously heard us.  But he would just sit there and stare as if he was just observing us or something.  I had always wanted a pet dog but this wasn't what I had been expecting.  I was thinking about a lovable cuddly puppy – something that would be adorable and cute, although even then I was not the kind of girl to carry a dog around in a little purse.  I did have this ideal of having a dog that would come and sit next to me on the couch, run to me when I got home from school and sleep at the foot of my bed.

With Emvee it was like we had a house guest, and we had to take care of him, like a small wolf we had inadvertently brought into our home.  Occasionally he followed us from room to room, watching us with intelligent eyes.  I could not imagine putting him in a little bag to carry around.  I was hesitant to put him on the leash.  He let me, of course, but I always got the feeling that he thought the leash was beneath him.  He submitted, but I could sense the disdain.

"Nah, just leave him this time," I answered in reply to Ken's question.  "I have to shop and we wouldn't want to tie him up outside."

Ken and I set out on foot.  Immediately, Emvee began to bark uncontrollably.  He was barking his head off.   He usually barked once or twice when we left for school, but this was bad.  He barked.  He howled.  He cried.  He pulled at his leash, desperate to go with us.  His hysterics were so bad that before we reached the end of the driveway I felt compelled to go back and make sure his chain would hold.  I thought he was going to break free and follow us.

"It's alright, boy," I reassured him, stroking his head. "We'll be back before you know it."

The minute I walked back to him, he was fine.

I've read that dogs have a sixth sense about some things. That dogs know an earthquake is going to hit long before humans do. Or that sometimes a dog will know when something bad is about to happen to his owner. A dog's senses are keener, and different, from our own. I guess with that heightened view of the world, he sees things that humans miss. In retrospect, I should have paid more attention to what Emvee was trying to tell me.

But I didn't. With absolutely no idea of what was about to happen to us, Ken and I left the house and started towards Omote-Sando.

We walked along the narrow streets that ran through the neighborhood. Before arriving in Japan, I had an image of Tokyo as futuristic land with tall skyscrapers. Crazy neon signs. That kind of thing. But that's not what our neighborhood was like. Around our house, there were very few buildings over two stories, and most of the homes appeared ancient to me. Narrow alleys meandered through the neighborhood, too skinny for a car to get through. You had to walk. High walls surrounded the homes and lined the streets. Wooden gates broke up the monotony of the walls. As we passed Ken and I looked between the cracks. Sometimes I could just get a glimpse of an old garden in front of a house.

We wound our way through the neighborhood until we got to the back entrance of the shrine. Meiji Shrine. It was a memorial shrine to the Meiji Emperor, surrounded by an enormous park. On this side of the shrine was our house. On the far side was Omote-Sando, a hip shopping district where I knew I could find the last-minute presents for the remaining people on my Christmas list.

Okay, actually I hadn't bought any presents at all. So the 'remaining people on my Christmas list' were the *only* people on my Christmas list. I had to shop for both Ken and Dad, but I figured I could knock that out in an afternoon without a problem. Having Ken with me might pose a challenge if I wanted the present to be a surprise, but I figured I could find a way to distract him. Christmas wasn't as big a deal for us now that mom was gone. Family events were not such a big deal either. Just a simple present would do the trick.

A narrow gravel pathway led through the grounds from the back of the shrine to the station on the other side. Thousands of people came to the shrine every day, but no one seemed to know about this pathway from the rear. Or perhaps they knew about it but never took it. Anyway, it was empty, and my brother and I found ourselves totally alone on the footpath.

We had only discovered the lonely route a few weeks ago and that was quite by accident. Looking to get into the adjacent park, we had stumbled upon it unintentionally. The entrance was quite obscure with no discernible sign and was easily missed. In fact, after discovering it, we had on more than one occasion returned to the same spot only to find that we had somehow missed the entrance and needed to walk around the entire circumference of the shrine, never finding our 'secret' pathway.

We enjoyed the gravel footpath precisely because it was so quiet and unused. Today was no exception. No one was around as we passed the huge pine and camphor trees that grew on either side of the path, blocking out the sun above us. The only sound we heard was from an evil looking crow with legs as thick as your little finger. It called out to us from the uppermost branches, adding to my gloomy mood.

Shortly after starting down the dark gravel pathway we came to a small guard hut. It was empty. The guard had apparently abandoned his post or perhaps there had never been a guard. The door was closed and the windows shuttered. A weathered signboard on the front of the hut offered a short explanation of the shrine, but it had faded away and was totally illegible.

Just beyond the abandoned guard hut was a *torii* – a huge wooden arch, soaring high above the gravel pathway. I knew nothing of its purpose, but the design alone was impressive. Two giant wooden columns, one on each side of the gravel, straddling the path we were on. The tree that donated these posts must have been enormous. Even if we had joined hands, Ken and I together could not have wrapped our arms around the circumference of one of those massive posts. An equally large beam went across the top, elegantly connecting the two columns. It arched gently upward at both ends, carved by some unknown craftsman many years ago. Over time, the life of the wood had faded. Now it was the color of driftwood, contrasting with the dark green of the trees around it. It was beautiful really. Sad. Old. Graceful. But I suppose at the time I never paused long enough to look at such things.

It was just at this moment that Ken called out to me.

"Hey, check this out!" he said from just off of the pathway. I stepped off of the gravel and went around the outside of the *torii*, wading out into a dreary pile of leaves. A short distance away from the path Ken poked the ground with a dirty stick.

"Looks like a small animal's tracks. Maybe a raccoon or a badger," he said. I could make out the faintest outline of sharp claws left in the mud. Considering this was the middle of Tokyo, it was unusual to find the tracks of some wild animal. I wondered if the shrine's wooded area could be large enough for an animal like that. But still sulking, I was in no mood for such distractions.

"Yeah great. Whatever," I griped and got back on the gravel pathway. "Come on. Let's go." I pushed passed him and started around the outside of the *torii*. Instead of going through the great wooden columns and under the graceful beam of the *torii*, I went around the outside.

We moved down the lonely path through the shrine. It was only late morning, but the weak sun was high in the sky – as high as it would get this time of year before giving up and starting its descent. The trees above our heads blocked the winter rays, blotting out our light, and the path we were on became darker and creepier as we walked on. The winter light made everything gray as if all color and joy had been washed out of the world.

When we rounded a bend, a cold wind blew along the pathway, rustling the shriveled leaves that made a hollow sound as they moved to escape. I shivered.

"Feels like everything here is sick," I told Ken. For some reason, it gave me the creeps. The air was thick and cold as I pushed ahead of my brother. My mind should have been on my shopping, but my heart was feeling as dark as the path we were on.

It was eerie to come across such a secluded spot in the middle of Tokyo. It was as if time had stopped and this place had never developed like the rest of the city. I strained my ears, listening for the sounds of the outside world, but heard only the crows calling to each other in their ominous language.

"Kaw. Kaw. Kaw." And then silence. Even the crows stopped talking. Everything was quiet. Graveyard quiet.

That's when I heard a gurgling noise behind me. It was a weird sound, even for my brother – a sound I could not identify. Like a growl that had come from deep in his stomach.

"Didn't you get enough to eat for breakf..." My words abruptly trailed off when I turned around.

Standing behind my brother was a creature unlike anything I had ever seen before. It was crouched to the side of the path, and at first, I thought it was a bear or some kind of gorilla.

10

'Or maybe it's been disfigured,' I thought to myself. But even as I considered these options, I knew it was none of these things.

The creature made the guttural sound again and sprung into motion. First it stood up. It had appeared large before, but now it was easily twice as tall as my brother. Its massive body was capable of enormous harm. Standing on stubby legs, it had huge disproportionately long arms that nearly touched the ground. Each arm was thicker than my waist, muscular and ready to strike. Its hide was hairless and...blue. Rough and covered in bumps, it reminded me of a leathery blue rhinoceros.

If the monster's body was frightening, its head was even worse. Two ugly blue horns curled on each side of its head, like a ram's horns that went back and around, ending in two malevolent points. Its face was distorted in an ugly sneer and sharp teeth protruded up from its lower jaw. It was horrible – the stuff of nightmares – and unlike anything I had ever seen before. But the worst part was the monster's eyes. Mean yellow eyes set in its blue skull. They were hollow and empty – not a flicker of compassion – and right now its brutal stare was focused right on me.

Our eyes locked, but my body was frozen in fear. My legs were made of lead. I felt light-headed, and for a moment I thought I might pass out.

Before I knew what was happening the monster used one of its huge arms to sweep my brother out of the way. Ken cried out as the monster effortlessly swept him aside. Then it charged past him, hurtling toward me with incredible speed and covering the distance between us almost instantly. I'd never seen any animal move that fast before, especially something of this size. With it this close to me, I was able to better gauge its proportions. It was enormous. It had brushed Ken out of the way like a rag doll, and now it towered over me.

The creature reached for me, grabbing me with one of its massive blue hands. Long dirty blue talons on its fingers, each one sharp and lethal looking, easily wrapped around me and began to lift me up towards an enormous gaping mouth. I could sense the sharp claws –dangerously close – but they didn't gore me. It lifted me off the ground, and I got an up-close glimpse of its impossibly sharp teeth.

The creature had me in a tight grip around the waist, but my hands were free and I tried to push its fingers down, thinking I could wiggle myself free from its powerful grasp. It was no use. Its fingers were solid and its hold on my body and legs was powerful. My fingers felt like they were pushing on blue concrete. I wasn't going anywhere.

Closer to its mouth, I could smell its breath. It was awful and reminded me of the garbage when we had left chicken in there too long. I wanted to gag but the monster's grip on me was so tight I could hardly breathe. I remember thinking incredulously, 'It is going to eat me.' My eyes were riveted on its gaping mouth. My face was just inches away now, and I could see its shark-like teeth set in rows in its blue gums.

'This is it,' I thought and closed my eyes.

Suddenly the creature made a different kind of noise. Was that an expression of pain? It was like a yelp. I opened my eyes.

The monster closed its mouth and turned from me to look to its left. It was a man with...an umbrella? It was a long black umbrella with a black handle. No, that wasn't right. It was something else. I squinted. The umbrella was blurry. Out of focus. I tried to look at it, but when I did my eyes hurt and I had to look away. I tried to take it in again. No, it wasn't an umbrella. It was a sword.

The man swung the weapon down quickly on the monster's left hand. He missed the wrist but caught the creature's finger. The umbrella/sword must have been incredibly sharp because it cut its flesh like it was going through butter. One of monster's fingers fell off onto the pathway. The creature bellowed in rage. Blue slime oozed out of where the finger had been. Confused for a moment, it dropped me to reach for its injured hand and stepped back in surprise.

You know how they say time slows down when you are under stress or in a car accident? For me, time stood still. I noticed the oddest details. I found myself looking at the Japanese fighter's shoes. They were made out of wood.

"Now that's odd," I thought.

They looked like old fashioned Japanese shoes, *geta* – a wooden base tied to his foot with a thong. But the fighter moved confidently in them – every step smooth and graceful.

The monster recovered from the blow and looked even angrier now. It swung at the fighter in rage, but he dodged nimbly out of the way of the sharp talons and swung his sword at the creature again. The blade narrowly missed the monster's throat, and it snarled savagely in response to the attack.

Suddenly, another man jumped in to help the first fighter. He was a lot older but dressed the same way. He had a sword too.

The two battled the creature with incredible ferocity, but it was unbelievably quick. They almost got it on every swing but it always managed to twist out of the way or pull an arm back just in the nick of time.

I was glued to my location watching in disbelief at the battle taking place before my eyes. Inside my chest it felt like my heart had stopped beating, as if it was afraid to be heard. I held my breath, unwilling to make a sound. I wanted to disappear into the ground. I wished I could hide. I thought of burying myself with dirt, camouflaging my body with the ground itself. Without warning, the fighting shifted and the monster and the two fighters headed my way.

The younger sword fighter yelled something at me in Japanese. I was taking Japanese class in school. I wasn't that good, and I'm not sure I knew the words he was saying, but on some level, I knew he was telling me to run. He didn't have to tell me twice. Whereas I had been rooted to the ground by fear before, now I felt fueled by a surge of adrenaline. I took off like a shot, heading for some bushes nearby. The monster used the moment that the fighter was distracted with me. It swung his arm with a backhand and connected with the fighter, who went flying across the path, crashing into a tree. He fell to the ground and didn't get up, knocked unconscious by the force of the blow. The creature bellowed its triumph.

Seeing the younger fighter fall, the older one redoubled his efforts to subdue the monster. He did a back roll and tried to stab its blue leathery skin with his sword. The thing spun quickly, dodged the sword and kicked the older fighter, sending him flying.

Turning its morbid attention back to me, the monster sprang towards the place where I was hiding. It was sniffing, smelling me out. I held my breath. Vulnerable. It was almost on me. The bushes offered inadequate protection, and the creature pawed at them with its talons, sensing my proximity. My heart was beating loud in my ears. I thought I was a goner. I thought I should try to flee, but even in my agitated state I realized I could never outrun this thing.

From the corner of one eye, I saw the young warrior still unconscious, crumpled at the foot of a tree a ways off from where I was hiding. His forsaken sword on the ground at his side. The monster's body towered directly over me, radiating evil. I could actually feel its evil intentions emanating from its body.

Suddenly, a rock the size of my fist flew through the air and hit it on the side of the face. A rock that size would easily have shattered my skull, but the monster only cocked its head. It was perturbed but not injured – not even dazed. Grunting its displeasure, it shook its head.

'What kind of creature can take such a beating?' I wondered.

The awful blue monster turned to look for the source of the rock, no doubt thinking about its next meal. To my surprise, I saw that it was Ken! He threw another rock and then another. Each came smashing in on the monster's head and face. Growling, it moved to stomp this little rock-throwing annoyance. Moving with unbelievable speed, it crossed the uneven terrain of the park in milliseconds. Almost immediately it was inches from where Ken was standing. It was unbelievably fast. Mind-bendingly fast. My stomach sank. I was about to see my brother eviscerated by this blue monster.

It was at that moment that the old man reappeared from behind a tree. He was back! Before the monster could touch Ken, the fighter attacked. He shoved Ken backwards to safety and catapulted himself forward towards his blue enemy. His sword arm shot out. I saw a flash of steel and the blade went deep into the monster's hand. Blue monster goo spattered out of the skewered appendage, and the monster howled in pain. It spun away from Ken, holding its injured arm close to its body.

Wounded, it darted over to a tree that had a small hole in its base. The hole was only big enough for a squirrel or maybe a small cat, but the monster reached his hand into it and pulled the edge of the opening to one side. It got bigger. I couldn't believe my eyes. The hole in the tree actually got bigger. It was pulling the edges of the opening, making it larger. It pulled an edge again and the opening grew further still. A moment ago, the hole had been impossibly small for this gargantuan monster, but now his head could easily fit. It squeezed its horns into the opening and pushed the rest of its body through, just as the old fighter reached the tree with his sword. The monster snarled savagely, pushed itself into the hole and narrowly escaped.

I had forgotten to breathe. Looking down at my shaking hands, I found myself panting and extremely agitated.

"Did you see that?" I asked Ken breathlessly. "What was that thing?"

"Blue *oni*," came the answer, but it wasn't from Ken. It was the old man. His voice was deep and gravely. "Japanese troll."

"Wh- wha- What?" I stammered. My mind was blank. I struggled to breathe. I wanted to either scream or cry and was worried I might pass out.

"Thanks for saving our lives," my brother said to the man. Ken was infinitely calmer than me. I stared at him. Had he seen the same monster that I had? How could he be so cool? He was breathing hard from the exertion but steady as he spoke.

"What was that thing?" I finally managed to get out. My voice was pinched and squeaky. My hands were shaking, and I was in danger of hyperventilating. I wasn't sure how to react. I choked back tears. I hated crying in general, and I *really* hated crying in front of strangers.

"Her name is Maya," Ken said covering for me. "My name is Ken." How could he stay so relaxed? I gulped air furiously, trying to force myself to calm down.

"Nice to meet you," said the old man. "My name is Kanbei." He bowed, steady and self-assured. He was older than my father, but he must have been in great shape. He wasn't breathing hard at all. Despite the close call, Kanbei had a feeling of eternal reassurance, making me feel like things were going to be okay.

"Just breathe," he said encouragingly to me. I nodded. It felt good to hear his calm voice, and I was glad he wasn't patronizing.

"I thought trolls were slow and stupid," I said my voice still quavering. This thing had been lightningning fast.

"No, Japanese *oni* aren't like that at all. They kill what they want," he said. His voice was serious.

The younger warrior with the ponytail came to join us, brushing leaves off his clothes unceremoniously. He was older than I was but not by much. I guessed him to be 18 or 19 years old. He didn't look much older than some of the kids in my high school. He stooped to pick up his sword. I watched him examine it momentarily and then slide it into its scabbard with one smooth motion. The sword was as casual a thing to him as a pencil was to me.

I heard him say, *"Moshi wake arimasen"* -- I am sorry. It was one of the few phrases that Ken and I knew. (We used it often.) The younger man bowed deeply to Kanbei. I assumed he felt bad because he had been knocked out. He had thrown himself into the fight without any hesitation, and I was embarrassed that he had been hurt trying to help me.

He held the bow for a long moment, waiting for Kanbei's response. I wondered what kind of reprimand he was going to receive. I studied the older warrior's face for some clue as to how he would respond.

If Kanbei was upset, he didn't show it. His face relaxed into a gentle expression and then quickly broke into a smile. I liked him immediately.

The two turned towards me and Ken, their hands still on the hilts of their swords.

"My name is Katsushiro," the younger one introduced himself to Ken and me with a formal bow. His face broke into a broad smile.

"It is unusual that the blue *oni* would attack you in broad daylight." Kanbei scratched his stubbly head as he spoke. His English was good, but I picked up his Japanese accent.

"Usually the *torii* and the gravel provide enough protection," Katsushiro explained to us.

"The *torii*?" Ken asked.

"The wooden gate that you came under at the entrance to the shrine. We put that there to offer protection to all that enter," Katsushiro told us.

"Protection?" I asked. I understood all the words he was saying, but nothing he said was making sense to me.

"Yes, the *torii* protects all who pass through it when they enter the shrine." Katsushiro told us in a casual tone as if it was the most natural thing in the world. He spoke as if he was talking about algebra or something as simple as a toaster. Sorry, I must have missed that subject in school.

"The gate protects us?" I asked, still trying to put together all the pieces.

Katsushiro graciously explained it again.

I looked at Ken, remembering the paw prints that he had called me over to see when we entered the park. "Um...I think we might have come in around the *torii*, not through it."

"That might explain it," Kanbei said slowly, thinking about the matter. "Still it is quite odd."

"Why does the *torii* offer protection?" I asked.

"The *oni* dislike the taste of meat that has gone through the torii," Katsushiro said matter-of-factly, as if the culinary preferences of blue *oni* were common knowledge. "The gravel pathway offers some additional protection. Usually that is enough. I don't know why this blue *oni* attacked you."

The two men were not sure why we had been singled out for attack. They were thinking about the 'why' while I was still struggling with what we had experienced.

"This is crazy. This kind of thing doesn't happen," I said unable to accept that I had just been nearly eaten by a troll. I was incredulous. The Japanese fighters assured me that it was very real but quickly moved on to next steps.

"We will escort you to the edge of the shrine. You should be safe after that."

I was still trying to get my mind around the idea of giant blue trolls coming up out of trees and attacking people. Ken, on the other hand, was totally fascinated by these two warriors. He was staring at their clothes.

"What are you guys?" Ken asked, pointing at the double swords they carried with them.

"We are samurai. We protect the peace." Kanbei straightened, pushing his shoulders back.

"Cool! Like Jedi?" Ken went on. I could have smacked him. I rolled my eyes and was about to yell at him when Kanbei replied.

He smiled. "Yes, like Jedi."

"I love that movie," Katsushiro nodded as he spoke, his eyes smiling.

Who were these guys? I wondered. What was the thing that attacked us? Ken relaxed now despite his recent brush with death, and these two men who claimed to be samurai were talking about this so calmly.

Actually, the samurai I could get my mind around. They must be some sort of reenactment club, a couple of harmless nerds who liked to dress up on weekends. Kanbei looked a bit old for that kind of thing, but hey, who was I to judge? But what about that monster? What was that thing? How could something like that exist in Tokyo?

"Are there more *oni* like that one?" I finally asked, unable to get the horrible image of the monster out of my head.

The samurai looked at each other. Kanbei's smile vanished, and he nodded in response. "Lots." His eyes were very serious. I shuddered.

"Lots?" I asked, nervously scanning the landscape around us. Suddenly it didn't seem safe anymore. I had been worried that the creature would come back, but now I wondered if there were others nearby. I studied my surroundings cautiously. I began to get the creepy feeling I was being watched.

"It is best that we get you out of here now," Kanbei instructed. He looked around. He wasn't nervous, but I could tell he was alert. I nodded quickly. I wasn't about to argue with him there. I was ready to get as much distance between me and that – that – that thing! – that blue *oni* as I possibly could. With that we started again down the gravel pathway again towards the Omote-Sando side of the shrine.

"We will get you out of the shrine and then you will be safe. You should avoid this and all other shrines in Japan," Kanbei instructed us.

"Do *oni* only come out in shrines?" Ken asked.

"No, not only shrines. But there is old magic in the ground where these shrines are built. The *oni* use that magic too," Katsushiro explained. Of the two, he was more eager to talk than Kanbei, more willing to tell us about the *oni* and what we were up against. "The power of these places is long forgotten. People just don't remember why they are important."

My legs were unsteady as I started walking. My mind was reeling from all this information. I felt my jacket were the *oni* had grabbed me, noticing the fabric was torn all the way through and something blue and slimy covered my sleeve.

"Oh gross," I groaned.

"What?" Ken asked.

"It is all slimy where that thing licked me," I said.

The samurai who were walking next to us suddenly stopped. They turned to look at me in unison.

"What did you say?" Kanbei asked, now no longer smiling. His voice had an edge to it that it hadn't had a moment ago.

"Yeah, I think it licked my jacket," I answered. I fingered the tear in my jacket and looked to see that my skin was okay.

"It licked you? Or it licked your jacket?" he asked, obviously wanting me to be exact in my answer.

I was a little freaked out after having a twelve-foot *oni* attack me and this line of questioning wasn't making me feel any better. What difference did it make? I had *oni* slime on my jacket. How precise did he expect me to be? The difference seemed unimportant.

"I'm not sure...uh..."

"It is really important. Try to remember. Did you feel it lick you?" Katsushiro wanted to know. His voice was urgent. "Did you feel its tongue?"

"Um..." I hesitated. The two samurai came over and examined the tear in my jacket. My entire sleeve was covered in a sticky blue *oni* spit ball, but I could not remember if the creature had licked before or after the jacket ripped. I didn't remember the feel of *oni* tongue but the whole thing had happened so quickly.

"What difference does it make if it licked her?" Ken asked.

"If the *oni* has tasted you it will never forget."

"It has your DNA signature," Katsushiro explained. "The monster will never rest until it has eaten you. There is no place in Japan where you will be safe. It will pursue you forever."

"What? I thought you said we were going to be okay? You said we just had to get out of the shrine," I said, starting to panic.

"That was before we knew it had tasted you," Kanbei replied.

"Well, we're not sure right? Maybe it just licked the jacket," I stammered in my defense.

The two samurai discussed the situation in Japanese. I could only understand a few words, but it sounded like Kanbei wanted to be safe and not take any chances. For the first time since the attack I thought of my father. How would I ever explain this to him? Hey, Dad, guess what happened to me today? I was attacked by a 12-foot troll and now I have to leave the country forever.

"We can't risk it." Kanbei said at last. "We have to take you to Kabuki-za. The magicians there will know what to do."

"Oh, we've been there," Ken volunteered. "It is the theater, right?"

Our father had taken us to a matinee one Saturday soon after we arrived. The play was long and extremely stylized. The theater building was memorable.

"Theater on the top floors," Kanbei said enigmatically. The way he said it made me wonder what was on the floors below ground.

"We will take you as far as the Palace," he continued. "The Imperial Guard will help you get to Kabuki-za. I hope that the magicians there can tell if you were licked by the *oni*."

What if they can't help me? I wondered silently but didn't dare ask it out loud.

19

"We must move quickly. Now time is of the essence." No sooner were the words out of Kanbei's mouth than he and Katsushiro had set out along the gravel path. Ken and I ran to catch up with them. They moved quickly in their wooden *geta*.

I looked at my brother. "What should we do?" I mouthed the words as we trailed along behind the samurai.

"Maya, we have to trust them," Ken reasoned. I nodded but wasn't quite so sure.

"Stranger danger, Ken." I whispered to him urgently. "What did we know about these guys in crazy samurai getup? Should we really be walking off with two guys we just met?"

Ken answered, "I think our only choice is to trust them."

"I'm not convinced."

"The danger from those blue *oni* is too great, Maya. We don't know anything about those creatures. And you saw how dangerous they were. It almost ate you."

"We almost died," I agreed. "But what do we know about these guys?" I tried to be practical. I was the older sister and I didn't like Ken calling the shots.

"Maya, they risked their lives to save us back there," Ken said logically. "Why would they do that if they meant us harm?"

I had to agree with him.

"You're right," I finally relented. As the morning slipped away, we sped up the pace, following our new friends, the samurai.

Chapter Two
Shopping on Omote-Sando

I remember that when we walked out through the *torii* at the main entrance of Meiji Shrine I looked up to see the winter sun. The sight made me feel immediately grateful to be alive. The air was cool, but I was not cold after the exertion of the walk and the faint sun warmed my skin. After being in the shade of the trees within the shrine, I was glad to be out in the open again. The experience with the *oni* had been my first time to feel so close to danger. An immense feeling of relief came over me. Little did I know how much danger lay ahead.

Above me, the crows – their dark forms silhouetted against the sky – flew in a peculiar pattern. I recall thinking that I had never seen crows behave in such a way before, and it made me uneasy. It gave me the uncomfortable feeling that the world was out of order, that things were not working the way they were supposed to.

In effect, we were traveling through the shrine in reverse, coming in through the rear entrance and now exiting through the front. As we passed under the huge wooden pillars that framed the road on this side of the shrine, I could not help but remember what Kanbei had said about "meat that has gone through a *torii*".

"I wonder if I'll feel different?" I thought to myself as I walked through the shadow of the thing, but if anything changed, I did not feel it. Beside me, the samurai made a curious gesture as they exited through the *torii*.

21

Thinking about the massive *oni* I had encountered, I briefly imagined what would have happened if I had become a meal for the monster. I shuddered. The stench of its breath when it pulled me close to its mouth clung to me. I could not shake it. I looked around anxiously, worried that perhaps the monster had followed me. When something stirred in a bush close to the path, my eyes shot to the spot, but it was only a small bird lurking in the shadow of the bush – nothing to worry about. My nerves were on edge.

In front of me, the broad welcoming expanse of Omote-Sando stretched out in front of the shrine. The street was crowded with Japanese couples and friends, laughing and holding hands. They peered into stores, chatting with one another. Cars waited at lights on the busy street. A taxi door swung open and a young woman with red heels stepped out. It was a scene of normal activity. People were busy doing the normal stuff of their lives. Even those normal things were strange to me now. Didn't those people know how close they were to danger? I briefly remembered the shopping plans I had made this morning, but Christmas seemed a long way away now.

At the time, I didn't know – or perhaps didn't much care – that *Omote* means "front" and *Sando* is "the path one follows to worship". The idea was that Omote-Sando provided a stately approach to the shrine for arriving visitors, a broad welcoming path for worshipers. Even that was messed up for me. My "worship" in the shrine had been an experience I had barely survived. Now my only thought was to get as far away from the place as I possibly could.

Years later, I learned that the boulevard had been created for the funeral procession of the beloved Emperor Meiji in 1912. I had seen videos of that on YouTube. They were some of the earliest movies from Japan, herky-jerky black-and-white images depicting the Emperor's mortal remains drawn by oxen. You can see the mourners gathered on the street in silence.

The samurai were concerned – perhaps 'obsessed' might be a better word – with their sense of place. It motivated them, anchored them in the cosmos. In time, I would learn to appreciate the history of an area. On that day, however, as we marched out of the shrine, it was the farthest thing from my mind, and the only 'mortal remains' I was thinking of were my own.

Ahead of us, the samurai walked together away from the shrine and conversed in Japanese with serious expressions. Ken and I walked a pace behind them. I was surprised that no one stared at them in their strange attire. They were clearly dressed as samurai and each carried two swords which protruded from their belts.

"You think that is a common sight in Tokyo?" I asked Ken.

"What's that?"

"Guys dressed like that," I said, pointing at them with my chin.

"I've never seen people dressed like samurai before," Ken said.

"Why don't people stop and stare?"

He shrugged.

I caught the reflection of our quartet in the window of a clothing store as we passed by. Kanbei and Katsushiro in front. Ken and I behind. We made an odd group: two Japanese guys with swords and two normal-looking American kids. Not what you see every day in Tokyo.

I turned from our reflection to the samurai walking in front of me and studied Kanbei's grey attire. He wore a solid charcoal *kimono* shirt without buttons. One side folded over the other. Perhaps it had once been black, but over time it had been washed and had faded to its grey color. His wide sleeves fell just above his wrists. His pleated *hakama* pants were tied high on his waist and hung loosely billowing when he walked. The *geta*, the wooden clogs on his feet which I had found so riveting during the attack, made a clip-clop sound as he walked along the concrete of the fashionable street.

Katsushiro was wearing the same kind of *kimono* as Kanbei, but it was less faded. His *hakama* was darker too, tied at his waist. He was lean, strong, and looked like an athlete to me. He had certainly moved like one when I watched him fight the monster. His jet-black hair was pulled back into a neat ponytail, bouncing as he walked. Walking behind him and to the right, I wondered if he was handsome. He had a strong jaw and smooth tanned skin.

"He is," I thought to myself, "But not in a Greek god sort of way."

"Where are we going?" Ken called out to Kanbei, interrupting my train of thought.

"We need to get you to the Hanzomon gate of the Emperor's Palace." Kanbei's voice was calm. Even in these small things, he inspired me with his confidence, taking the edge off my worry. There was a calmness, a serenity, to the way he led us.

I don't say these things to persuade you one way or another about Kanbei. I just want you to understand how it is that Ken and I came to trust our lives into his hands. There was something in his demeanor that made us follow him as he led us towards the Palace.

If there was any lingering doubt in Ken's mind about the samurai, he didn't show it. He pulled out the phone that had been a gift from Dad earlier that year for his birthday. I had received one the year before, but mine sat on my dresser at home. I was not the technology buff that Ken was – although I thought briefly about my Candy Crush addiction – but I was glad that he had brought it with him this time. It felt like a tether to the life that I remembered – our normal life. Ken punched "Emperor's Palace" into the map on his phone. A blue line popped up indicating the recommended route.

"Are we taking the subway?" he asked, looking at the map. His phone showing him this was the quickest way.

"No, it is too dangerous. *Oni* live underground. They frequently use the subway tunnels," Kanbei explained.

"Also, subway conductors work with the *oni*," Katsushiro added. His tone was serious, bordering on angry. He clenched his jaw after he spoke.

"They work with those monsters?" I asked incredulously.

"Yes," Kanbei answered but then said nothing else. His face was tense. Ken and I blinked expectantly at him waiting for further explanation, but we didn't know what to ask.

Reading our expressions, Katsushiro spoke up, "Sometimes they will stop the subway. They announce an accident or that someone isn't feeling well on the train. Then a few station personnel will pull a person off the train. They take that person to an underground room in the subway station. That's where the handover tales place."

"They hand people over to those monsters?" I could not believe what I was hearing. The thought sickened me.

"Yes."

Kanbei frowned at Katsushiro.

"What? She needs to know," the younger samurai answered in reply to Kanbei's sharp look.

I got the feeling that there was a lot more that they weren't telling us. The world was a stranger, darker place since the attack in the shrine. Who would cooperate with an evil monster like that? What kind of person would do such a thing? I had been on subways that stopped for a passenger who was ill and had heard the announcements. I had never seen the *oni* and could hardly believe that such an atrocity was taking place in modern Tokyo. What else had I not seen?

"Let's just say it is better that we stay out of the subway system," Kanbei told us, bringing an end to the discussion. He spoke with an authority and we didn't dare to question him.

"So, we taxi?" I asked.

"It is better that we walk."

"It is good to have lots of people around," Katsushiro explained. "The *oni* are less likely to attack in the open. They don't like crowds."

"So, we walk?" Ken asked, hoping there was another way.

Kanbei nodded his shaved head.

Ken punched a button on his phone. "That will take us hours," he moaned.

"My brother the wimp," I thought.

"It shouldn't take us more than two," Kanbei corrected. He had a sense of command. I thought he was used to giving orders and having them obeyed. He didn't come across as haughty though. On the contrary, he seemed quite kind and smiled a lot when he spoke. It's just that I could tell he was accustomed to being in charge, comfortable with his authority.

"I could follow a person like this," I thought to myself.

"So, we walk," I said, elbowing Ken. "No big deal." I hoped he would take it as encouragement, but he shot me a dirty look as if I was the one who had forced this upon him.

"First we need to get some supplies," Kanbei told us. I guessed that this is what the two had been discussing in Japanese earlier. I was glad that the samurai were helping us prepare. The idea that they were going to take care of us was comforting to me, and I desperately needed a little comfort. Actually, I had no idea what supplies we were going to need for a two-hour walk, but I was just glad that someone else was thinking about the details for me.

Katsushiro explained this to us as well.

"We are going to need to...uh... suit you up," he said. I wondered at the pause in his sentence. I think he had hoped to stop there but when he saw the clueless looks on our faces and knew that we had no idea what he was talking about, he tried to amplify for our understanding.

"We want you to wear some," he paused again, "Protective... er... clothes."

I could not tell if he was searching for the right word in English or if he was avoiding telling us something.

"Armor?" Ken asked. Catching on quickly and immediately forgetting the bleak prospect of the long walk, he was suddenly excited. "We get to wear armor?"

Katsushiro nodded looking down at the ground. Kanbei looked the other direction. He wasn't smiling. I could see now that he hadn't wanted to tell us about the armor. I was sure he was doing it so that we wouldn't be frightened. I resolved to not be afraid about this. But to be honest, I did not feel at all brave. Far from it. My heart felt like wax inside my chest. However, Kanbei and Katsushiro had risked their lives to save me as Ken had pointed out earlier, and even now they continued to work to help us. I resolved to do my part. From somewhere deep within me I summoned the courage to take the next step.

Ken didn't seem to have the same reservations that I had. For him, armor was a thrill.

"Did you hear that, Maya? We get armor." His excitement was palpable.

At home I had always thought of myself as the practical one in our family. Since Mom was gone, a lot of the day-to-day tasks fell to me. I was accustomed to thinking things through. Now I wondered where we were going to find armor. One does not simply walk into 7-11 and pick out Japanese armor. Was there some kind of Japanese weapons emporium nearby?

"Here," Kanbei said as if answering the question in my mind. We had stopped in front of a used clothes store on Omote-Sando. A neon palm tree flickered in the window and a cardboard sign read:

*Used clothes. All jeans 50% off.*

"Not what I was expecting," I said and followed the samurai inside.

The store was in the basement, down a flight of stairs. Used clothes of every style and fashion lined the walls. Young Japanese people congregated in the aisles, trying on clothes and looking in mirrors. Every available space was filled with some kind of used clothing. We walked past leather jackets, denim jackets, and wool sweaters. The store had seemed tiny at first, but then we turned a corner at what I thought was the back wall and I saw that it kept going. We pushed past dresses and denim jeans. Past scarves and sleeveless shirts.

"Wow, this place has everything," I said.

"Yes," Kanbei agreed and smiled again.

We pushed past a group of Tokyo teen agers – two boys and two girls – who were looking at rack of flannel shirts, chatting with each other amiably in Japanese. I understood only a word here and there, but I imagined in my mind what they must be saying. 'This looks good on you', 'No, it's too small' – it was a world of fashion and friends that I had barely discovered. And now I might never get to know it. I was one blue *oni* attack away from annihilation. I sighed, briefly worried that I would never know a normal childhood.

We turned another corner and this time found the Japanese clothes. I saw shelves stacked with piles of *kimono*. Each shelf was labeled. Wedding *kimono*. Formal *kimono*. *Kimono* for summer. *Kimono* for winter. I noticed there were a lot fewer people here. A few foreigners shopped for souvenirs. The Japanese mostly congregated in the front looking at the western clothes. We passed piles of *obi*, Japanese sashes, which covered another row of shelves.

"This way," Kanbei led us further into the store.

He took us down an aisle to an area behind the *kimono* section. At first, I thought we had reached a door, and for some reason I thought it said "staff only", but as we followed Kanbei closer I realized there was no sign...there wasn't even a door.

"That's weird," I said to Ken. My eyes must have been playing tricks on me. It just seemed like it *should* have been an area for employees only.

"What's weird?"

"Wasn't there a door right there?"

"Maya, I don't know what you're talking about," he said eagerly looking around, barely listening to me.

I followed Kanbei closely. His feet in wooden *geta* shoes made a 'clip-clop' sound on the black and white tiled floor. As we pushed deeper into this section of the store I saw racks arranged six feet high and piled with every conceivable type of samurai armor. There were no bullet proof vests or flak jackets. It was ancient Japanese samurai armor, helmets and swords arranged neatly in racks.

"Wow!" was all Ken could say, thrilled by the sight of the weapons. He turned and disappeared quickly down an aisle. Less enthusiastic, I went on ahead.

Each aisle had shelves, and each shelf was stocked with every kind of war implement one could imagine. Some of it I recognized. Certainly, I had seen something similar in a museum or in a book someplace. Other pieces were more obscure. I paused to look at the various helmets. The first one I came to had metal plates woven together with silk cords. Next to that was a majestic helmet which boasted scars from some ancient battle. This one was plain looking. That one had an elaborate dragon ornamentation on the forehead. Another had a decoration with a golden tiger raising its paw, its jaws open as if it were roaring.

Behind the helmets was a small raised platform made of wood with a woven *tatami* mat resting on it. On the *tatami* was a purple pillow and on the purple pillow was an old man. From his perch he had an excellent view of the shop floor. He was so quiet when we entered that I had failed to notice him. When I caught sight of him out of the corner of my eye, it startled me. I must have jumped.

"Oh, hello," I said.

He said nothing but bowed from his seated position. His head went low, almost touching the purple pillow he was sitting on. I wondered if he spoke English. He looked ancient. I smiled and tried a bow. His position on the pillow gave him a great vantage point.

"I bet you can see everything from there," I said still unsure if he understood me. He bowed again. His eyes did not waiver. His face showed no emotion.

"Well, I'm just going to look over here," I said nervously pointing to an aisle over my shoulder. His composure unexpectedly made me unsettled.

I turned into the aisle behind me and ambled down it, gingerly touching the armor as I passed.

"Chose something that fits," was the only advice that Kanbei had given us. He said it with a serious look and then nodded in agreement with himself, letting us know that this was the only wise course of action. He needn't have worried about me, but Ken, on the other hand, lost all trace of restraint. He bolted off, plunging down one of the aisles with reckless abandon, scooping up armor in a frenzied rush as he went. I wished I had his enthusiasm.

Once when we were small – it must have been not long after Mom left – my father had taken us to a toy store. I remember it was shortly before Christmas, and the shelves were bursting with temptation. Dad told us to each choose one present.

"He is being optimistic," I had whispered to my brother, making us both laugh. Ken and I easily filled a shopping cart that day. I remembered our excitement, adding one toy after another to the cart. Dad had been so eager to make us happy that year, and we were more than willing to let him indulge us. Those seemed like happy times now. I smiled, remembering the shopping cart.

In my memory, Ken looked up at me with an ecstatic expression on his face. We laughed together, happy to be choosing our own presents. Although the toys were already piled high in the cart, we continued to find space for more.

On the shelf in front of me, I found my dream toy. I remember wanting it so badly that year. It was a Lego version of "Harry Potter." It was the Hogwarts Castle set, the big one with thousands of pieces. I picked up the box with both hands, eyeing the cover.

"This will never fit in the cart," I said to myself quietly. The toy was enormous. "Ken, move your stuff. Make room for this," I bossed.

Reluctantly, he moved one of his toys to make room for mine.

Suddenly, a blue hand reached up out of the toys in the cart like a jump scare in a movie. The hand was enormous with razor-sharp claws. Dirty talons were now only inches away from me. It was reaching right for me.

The toys fell away, falling out of the cart to the floor. As they fell to the ground, an *oni* emerged from the cart, lunging towards me. Its enormous body sprang from the cart like a great blue jack-in-the-box, springing right towards me.

I opened my mouth to scream, but nothing came out. My throat was dry and choked with fear. I tried to run, but my feet were anchored in place. Ken, who had been standing next to me only a moment ago, melted away behind me. I was left alone with the horrible *oni*, inches away from my face.

"Oh!" I gasped, blinking my eyes. Just as the *oni* in my imagination was about to grab me, I snapped back to reality. It was just a hallucination, a waking dream, but it had been so vivid, so real. The *oni* had begun to insert itself into my memories, infecting my mind like a virus. I didn't know it then, but the *oni's* poison would continue to contaminate my memories, one after another, slowly loosening my grip on reality.

Feeling confused, I looked around the shop for Kanbei and the others, trying to remember where I was. Dizzy and disoriented, I was concerned by the shocking violence of my own thoughts.

"Focus, Maya," I told myself, trying to shake off the infected memory. I knew at that moment I had to go with Katsushiro and Kanbei as quickly as possible. I could tell there was no time to lose. Like the onset of a cold when you can tell your body is getting sick, my body knew that something was terribly wrong. I had to go with them to the Palace as quickly as possible.

The room was not cold, but I shivered and set out to search the aisle for armor I could use. Fingering the tear in my sleeve where the blue *oni* had cut through the sleeve of my jacket, I decided to start by looking for something that I could wear on my arms. I had seen something somewhere. Where had that been? Retracing my steps, I discovered an assortment of arm protectors, which reminded me of the shin protectors I used in soccer practice. I held one up to my arm. It was for an adult man. Too large for me. I tossed it back and fumbled for another. This one appeared to be the right size but I could not see how to attach it to my arm. Did it lace up? Did I tape it to my arm?

I was still struggling with the left side when I heard Ken say, "Hey look, Maya."

What I saw made me laugh. Ken had lost no time in finding armor to wear. He had the same arm protectors I was considering, but he also had a sword in both hands, plus one tucked into his belt and a dagger strapped to his leg. Ill-fitting shoulder pads hung down lopsidedly, protecting his right arm slightly more than his left. On his back he sported some sort of a backpack with a spear that stuck up behind him like his own personal flagpole. He was ready for war. Somehow the image fit.

I thought of all the times I had called Ken "Mr. Volcano-head." I wasn't sure how I felt about discovering my kid brother so heavily armed. On one hand, I was glad to see him so well equipped for his own safety. On the other hand, I'd seen him get into many fights at school. I hated to think about what he would do if he was armed this way.

Just then Katsushiro approached, his *geta* announcing his presence with a clack-clack on the tiled floor. He took one look at

Ken and smiled. He didn't laugh. He didn't tease. He just folded his arms and looked at my brother.

"You have some excellent weapons there," he said after a moment.

Proud of his accomplishments, Ken grinned like a birthday boy who is convinced that the vast array of presents is thoroughly deserved.

Katsushiro went on. "Will you be able to walk to the Palace?" He asked it as a serious question with absolutely no trace of sarcasm.

"Uh...hmm...." Ken stammered. I could see him move his shoulders as he thought about walking for hours with the load. He shifted the weight of the backpack. The protruding spear slumping dejectedly to one side. Without responding to Katsushiro's question, he began to put some of the equipment down quietly. His reluctance to give up his weapons amused me.

I liked the way that Katsushiro was teaching Ken. His message was simple and sincere. It didn't sound like the scolding or mind-numbing criticism that we endured in school. I could see that Ken was absorbing it and learning quickly. Katsushiro had our best interests in mind, and our trust for him grew.

Kanbei came up behind us, scratching the stubble on his face. He had the smile on his face that I was becoming accustomed to seeing. His eyes twinkled when he saw Ken. Then he turned to consider me.

"I think we will need to protect more than your arm," he said, eyeing the protector which hung limply down by my elbow. "Katsushiro, help our friend find something appropriate, won't you?"

Katsushiro nodded, handing me some armor as if he had been expecting Kanbei's order.

"How about this?"

It was a *dou*, a chest protector. Looking like something a Japanese football player might have used 1000 years ago, it was padded on the inside and seemed like it would be warm. The outside was hard and black and shiny. The surface was coated in black lacquer. I tapped it with my finger nail and it made almost no sound, as if the armor was absorbing the vibrations from my tapping. I wondered if it was tough enough to protect me from a sword. Maybe even a bullet.

Katsushiro unhinged it for me, and I slipped it on. Blue cords went over my shoulders and connected to a piece that protected my back. I intuitively fiddled with the blue chords to adjust the size. It fit perfectly, accommodating my frame and causing me to briefly wonder if it had been designed for a woman. I felt comfortable wearing it.

I caught sight of myself in a mirror that hung on the wall. The combination of the chest protector and the arm guards was impressive. I looked like a warrior, although I didn't feel like one on the inside. "If only the kids at school could see me now," I thought to myself. I imagined walking into the cafeteria wearing the armor. With a sense of guilty pleasure, I allowed myself to fantasize about seeing the kids from my Algebra class.

It was that moment that Kanbei chose to give me my first sword.

The sword itself was beautiful – a three-hundred-year-old weapon, signed by its maker and protected in a black lacquer sheath. It was a little on the short side, but well balanced and – although I didn't know it at the time – perfect for my frame. The handle was wrapped in black material in an intricate diamond pattern and through the openings in the diamond pattern I could just make out a tiny carved dragonfly ornament.

Kanbei held the weapon out to me horizontally so I could grab it from both ends and said, "Katana," gesturing for me to take it. I hesitated for a moment, and then reached for it, but he held on for a moment longer. I waited but he didn't let go.

"One thing I want you to remember," he said deliberately, locking eyes with me. "When you pull this sword out of its sheath – no matter what the result – your life is going to change forever."

I nodded, although in all honesty, I had no idea at the time of how true his words would prove to be. The two of us held the sword there like that, poised as it was at the intersection between two futures. Finally, he let go, and I received the katana with both hands, holding it awkwardly. It was heavier than I had anticipated.

"Just don't drop it, Maya," I told myself.

Katsushiro, who was watching this, stepped up to me and showed me how to wear the weapon in my belt. I lifted my arms while he positioned the weapon in my belt for me.

I know. I know. If you were picking teams for samurai, I would be the last one you would pick. I had never used a samurai sword. I barely spoke a word of Japanese. And I had always thought of myself as a little bit clumsy. But here I was, dressed like a samurai. My life was in danger, and I was on the verge of the biggest adventure of my life. And you know the biggest thing on my mind right then?

"Won't people stare at us if we walk around in these kinds of outfits?" I whispered to Katsushiro, feeling a wave of self-consciousness overcome me. I should have felt thrilled to hold such a magnificent weapon in my hands. Instead I felt self-conscious. I turned to see how I looked from the back.

"You would be surprised at what people are capable of ignoring," Katsushiro replied. He shook his head, causing his ponytail to bob.

"It seems like we will stand out," I said, feeling suddenly awkward like the only one dressed for a costume party.

"Do you remember when you first saw me?" quizzed Kanbei who had overheard me.

I nodded.

"What was I wearing?"

I pictured the moment I had seen him coming towards me when the *oni* had attacked. "Uh, a grey sweatshirt...maybe a jogging suit." At first it had seemed so clear, but as I tried to recall the image, it became fuzzy in my mind. It became harder to remember the more I tried to focus on it, as if the memory squirmed out of view.

I tried replaying the scene in the shrine again, starting at the beginning and then fast-forwarding to the moment when Kanbei had appeared on the scene. In my mind's eye, I turned to look at him, but as I stared at him he seemed to recede. That part was fuzzy, and the more I thought about it the fuzzier it became. Without thinking, I blinked my eyes twice as if that would help me focus. Kanbei could see the confusion on my face as I tried to remember.

"Look at me now. What am I wearing?" he asked finally. His clothes were in fact grey but he was obviously wearing a Japanese *kimono*. He had a cloak with a hood that I had somehow mistaken for a sweatshirt, and those odd wooden clogs.

"I have not changed clothes," Kanbei said matter-of-factly. I could not figure it out and told him so.

"In the shrine, you saw what your mind told you to see," he explained for me.

"I remember you were carrying an umbrella!" I blurted out. That part was clear in my mind. I was glad to have at least one aspect of the story right. A self-satisfied smile crossed my face, but it was premature.

Kanbei held up his sword sheathed in its scabbard.

"You mean this umbrella?" he asked.

"It doesn't look anything like an umbrella," I admitted, feeling silly. I had been so sure it was an umbrella only a moment ago. How could I have missed that?

"It is the Blindness," Kanbei said.

I looked at him not understanding and feeling quite stupid.

"Don't worry, Maya," he said. "The more you practice, the more you will see things as they really are."

"How they really are?"

"The truth about the world we live in."

"This is how blue *oni* can still live in Tokyo." Katsushiro added.

"How can people not see those terrible creatures?" I asked, not ready to believe it.

"People cannot see what they refuse to believe."

I wondered if it this could possibly be true. Were there really armed samurai walking around Tokyo, but I had been too blind to see? Surely someone would notice if we went out of the store decked head to toe in samurai armor. People hadn't noticed when Kanbei and Katsushiro came walking out of the park, but surely that was just a fluke. Or perhaps the clothes looked more natural on them. It was tempting to believe them, but surely not everyone was that "blind".

"Still I would feel better if Ken and I could cover this up," I said at last, my self-conscious nature winning out. I refused to believe that we would go unnoticed.

To their credit the samurai made no attempt to argue or convince me further.

"How about wearing this?" young Katsushiro offered charitably. He handed Ken a long sleeve t-shirt. Ken pulled it on over his armor. The black long sleeve fit him perfectly. The shirt had blue dragons curling up his sleeves. The dragons circled his arms, breathing fire and flashing their sharp claws. An exotic design covered the lower half of the shirt. I could still see the outline of his armor under the shirt, but now he looked as if he had just stepped out of a video game.

"Cool!" Ken said. He really did look awesome.

"Here is one for you," Kanbei said and handed me a t-shirt. My face dropped when I held it up. It said, 'I heart Tokyo'.

"This?" I asked examining the shirt I'd been given. "I'll look like a tourist. Hey Ken, you wanna trade?"

"No, I'm good," he answered quickly.

Katsushiro laughed. It was a great laugh. He threw his head back and laughed without restraint. I liked it. Although I knew he was laughing at my situation, it didn't feel mean. There was a certain honesty about Katsushiro, a warmth. It felt like an authenticity of purpose. I believed he was there to protect me.

To tell you the truth, it's hard to remember Katsushiro exactly as I perceived him that day when we first met. I was terrified of the *oni* and those feelings colored my thinking as much as my worries about what others thought. I'm sure that so much of the way I remember him now has to do with the experiences we have shared since that day. When I shut my eyes and try to recall how I felt at the time, I realize my feelings were colored by our situation. The samurai had appeared out of nowhere to save me, and all of my hopes were pinned on them. Katsushiro was my guide, opening my eyes to a world that I had never seen before. I knew I should be grateful.

Still, I didn't like the t-shirt. I was about to protest, but then Kanbei brought it to an end when he ordered us: "Okay, time to go."

We grabbed the things we needed. I pulled the t-shirt over my head and picked up my things. Feeling self-conscious, I looked around for a mirror to examine my reflection again before we left. Not finding one close by, I relented and followed the samurai and Ken towards the exit. Little did I know that the armor – that same armor about which I was so self-conscious – was about to save my life.

Looking back over the years on the events of that day, I realize how silly I must have appeared to the samurai. Even in those dangerous circumstances, I was still concerned with what other people thought of me and how I looked. At the time they did not fault me for my odd behavior. Or if they did, they did not let on. Now my hair is grey, my face is as wrinkled as my hands, and I seldom worry about what others think of my appearance. But on that cold day in December – I remember it so well – I was concerned with how I looked in my armor, standing there with my *katana* stuffed awkwardly into my belt.

On the way out of the used clothing store in Omote-Sando, Katsushiro produced a small bag from his grey *kimono*. He pulled out a gold coin with a hole in it, but it was unlike any coin I had seen since we arrived in Japan. It was round but the hole in the middle was square. From my position behind Katsushiro, I could see the kanji characters on the surface of the coin around the square hole. He paid the old man who was still sitting silently on the pillow watching us. The old man bowed silently from his seated position, his head almost touching the ground.

When Katsushiro handed him the coin, the old man stuck out his hand. He had strong wrists, but his hands were covered with scars. I wondered what could have caused those scars. Then I remembered the blue *oni's* sharp teeth and shuddered.

With that we left the store and headed for the Palace.

Chapter Three
A Stroll Down Aoyama-dori

We left the used clothing store and walked into the cool outdoor breeze on Omote-Sando. Ken and I had our t-shirts on over our armor, but Kanbei and Katsushiro were only wearing their cloaks over their *kimono*. The handles of their long swords protruded out of their belts.

I watched the faces of the people we passed. No one stared. A couple holding hands almost bumped into Katsushiro.

"*Sumimasen*," sorry, the man said but never looked away from the young girl he was walking with. I heard two girls squeal as we walked by and thought, "We've been seen!" But their excitement was over something in a store window that we were passing. No one turned our way. No one stopped to stare. No one ran away screaming in fright at the site of our swords and armor. Most people never looked our way at all. And the ones who did glance at us, didn't seem to notice anything out of place, or at least said nothing.

A young child walking with his mother looked right at us and stopped dead in his tracks. He was wearing a huge blue jacket that made his arms stick out from his sides. His mouth fell open once he saw us, and he just lingered there quietly staring. I know he saw us. I mean, he really saw us.

"It isn't polite to stare," his mother told him and jerked his hand. She glanced at us, smiled weakly and pulled him away. She obviously didn't see or didn't notice our weapons.

37

That's how it went. Here we were, four people, heavily armed, wearing 300-year-old samurai outfits walking through the middle of the most fashionable district in Tokyo, and the only one who noticed us at all was a four-year-old.

I wondered if the Blindness had affected me the same way. Had I walked past samurai on my way to the bus stop? Was I too caught up in my own world to see what was really going on? I went down a checklist in my mind of the places I'd been. School. My neighborhood. The shopping district by my house. If I was missing this, what else might have happened that I had missed before? We walked along Omote-Sando as a group while I wondered about what else I had overlooked in my life.

The tree-lined boulevard ran down a gentle hill to an intersection, before changing its mind and starting a long slow incline, as if to support the adage that what goes up must come down – or perhaps disproving it. As we walked, Kanbei explained that the crosswalk at the bottom of the slope had long ago replaced the Shibuya River which once occupied that space. The crosswalk there had since become the inflection point for the street, which meant that pedestrians coming from either direction spent the first part of their stroll going downhill and the second half walking up the grade.

Around us was the appropriately named neighborhood of Jingumae. (*Jingu* means "shrine" and -*mae* means "in front of".) Ken and I had frequently visited Omote-Sando, but I wasn't a fan of Jingumae. The area was an urban planner's nightmare with crooked paths too narrow for cars, dead-end streets which appeared without warning and an anything-goes attitude to architectural design. We always got lost there. Omote-Sando was the reverse. The sidewalks were wide and calm, and the buildings along the street were arranged in a regimented row as if to hold back the crush of the dull gray buildings that jostled up against one another in Jingumae like some sort of architectural mosh pit.

I loved –no, that's not quite right– I *needed* the tranquility of Omote-Sando with its claim to higher purpose for those on their way to Meiji Shrine. Framed by graceful swaying *keyaki* trees – sorry, I've forgotten the name of the tree in English– Omote-Sando was a calm oasis for me now. The garish neon and gaudy flashing lights we had seen in the other parts of Tokyo were nowhere to be found along this boulevard, and I was glad for a moment of peace. It calmed me.

After a while we completed our walk up the slope with Meiji Shrine to our backs and came to the intersection where Omote-Sando begins. Two stone lanterns stood sentinel on either side of the street, where they had been since the inauguration of Meiji Shrine. On the corner was a small police station – more of a police box really, certainly no bigger than the smallest room in our house.

Two tough-looking police officers strutted in front of the box. One paused briefly to help a tourist who had dared ask for directions. The other put his thick hands on his hips, scrutinizing the pedestrians as they wandered by. I had been warned about the cops in Japan before. They were no-nonsense guys, keepers-of-the-peace who took their job extremely seriously.

"Uh-oh," I thought. "This is it. We are goners for sure."

I imagined myself getting arrested and telling the police why I was walking around in samurai armor with a couple of heavily armed bodyguards. I wondered if I'd be able to explain it in English, let alone in Japanese. *Oni*. Samurai. *Katana*. Yeah, right. In my mind I imagined the cops would get the samurai reference. And the *katana* was obvious, protruding as it was from my hip. How would I ever explain the *oni*? How would I get anyone to believe me about that?

I waited for some serious-looking cop to spring out of his police box and tackle us. Or at least to question us on our purpose for being so heavily armed. To my surprise, the uniformed cop faced us for a moment and then glanced away. I could not tell if he looked at us long enough to recognize what we were wearing or if the Blindness was so strong that he was just unable to take it all in.

Katsushiro saw me looking at the officer. He leaned over to me and whispered, "The Blindness can be a powerful ally." He smiled at me, resting his hand conspicuously on the handle of his sword.

The road we were walking along had four lanes and was well-paved. Shops lined the sidewalks on both sides and a wide area between street and building allowed ample room for pedestrians and bicycles.

Ken and I fell a step behind our samurai guardians. "I thought we would be arrested on sight," I told my brother. He said nothing but nodded.

"How could they miss us?"

"It's as if they couldn't see us at all," he replied, wondering about the experience as I had.

He pulled his phone out of his pocket and looked at the map on the device. I looked over his shoulder at the glowing screen.

"I think we just go straight here until we get to the Palace," he said, poking the screen with his index finger. The map on his phone indicated a straight-line path down the road we were on.

I peered into the windows of the shops that we passed. There were clothing stores and flower shops. One store sold bicycles. Another sold sporting goods. I thought for a moment about my plans to shop for Christmas presents. That felt like a long time ago.

Slowing down behind Ken, I peeked into an old-fashioned sweets store. They had the kind of Japanese cakes and candies that Ken and I had discovered soon after our arrival in Japan.

The store had an open front, which quickly gave way to a tranquil environment away from the hustle and bustle on the street outside. I poked my head in, ducking under the awning. There was no door to speak of, and I briefly wondered what they did when the weather was bad. The shop was quiet, and there was no sign of the shopkeeper. The dim lighting made me wonder if it was closed, but in the glass display case freshly-made sweets caught my eye.

"Mmmm. Japanese sweets. My favorite," I thought, realizing I hadn't eaten since breakfast.

If it was like the shop in our neighborhood, they would have *kuri-mushi*, a sweet made with sweetened chestnuts. My favorite was a particular kind of *mochi*, a rice cake that reminded me of Turkish Delight. My stomach growled.

I was just ready to duck out of the shop and catch up with my brother when I noticed five or six porcelain cats placed in the window, facing the street. My brother and the samurai had not stopped but they were not far ahead. I knew I could catch up. They were only five or six paces ahead of me. I lingered in front of the porcelain cats.

"Oh, we learned about these in school. *Maneki-neko*," I said out loud to no one in particular.

I stopped to look at the cats more carefully. They were different sizes – three white cats and two black ones. The largest was about the size of an actual house cat. Each one had one paw raised as if waving. I knew this was a sign of good fortune. The cat's raised paw supposedly brought in prosperity. Our teacher had said that shopkeepers placed these porcelain *maneki-neko* in their stores to ensure good business.

They were so well crafted. So realistic. Then, as I looked at them, one of the black cats seemed to move. I blinked. Had I just seen that? It was just outside my field of vision. Just out of my perception. I looked again carefully. Surely not. Porcelain cats don't move, do they? My eyes darted from cat to cat. I examined each carefully again. Nothing.

"You're seeing things, Maya," I told myself. Porcelain cats don't move.

I studied each cat, starting with the whites. The whites sat on red pillows. They had exquisitely painted red collars and little porcelain bells around their necks. The one on my far left clutched a hand-painted porcelain coin under one paw. Standing steady in front of them, I scanned one cat and then moved on to the next one to the right, searching for any sign of movement. Each cat was solid porcelain, shiny and clean. I looked methodically from the first cat. Then to the second cat.

Twitch.

There it was again. On the far right. Had it moved? I just caught it out of the corner of my eye. It was the faintest sense of motion from the black cat in the back. It was subtle, the faintest swish of its whiskers.

Now I was transfixed, determined to catch it in the act. I turned to stare at the black one that had moved. Porcelain. I focused on the whiskers for a moment. No movement. My gaze moved up to the porcelain ears. Nothing. I could almost see my own reflection in its shiny black porcelain skin. But then there were the eyes. The eyes were yellow, almost glowing, and for just an instant, the cat seemed to smile. The corners of its mouth curled up in a wicked grin. I planted my feet and stared at the black one, waiting for it to move again.

"It's my mind playing tricks on me," I thought. "Probably the sun glinting off a car in the street behind me." I knew that porcelain cats don't move.

I focused on the cat and held my breath. Staring.

Twitch.

I had been ready for it this time. My heart leapt, but my body stayed put. This time the cat really did move. As I stared at it, the cat licked its lips and twitched its whiskers. I blinked twice and stared hard at the cat. I leaned forward to have a better look. I imagined – but didn't dare attempt – lifting the cat to me.

"Little porcelain kitty," I whispered, leaning forward.

Without warning, the cat hissed at me, its open mouth revealing surprisingly sharp-looking teeth. Its porcelain lips curled back in a feline snarl. Taken aback, I straightened. The cat turned and disappeared behind the other (still porcelain) cats. I thought I could see the long black tale swishing behind the cats as it moved.

"Why you wicked little kitty," I said.

I leaned to the left to see where it had gone, looking around the frozen white cats with their bells. Careful to keep my distance this time, I felt a vague sense of unease come over me. What had animated this little porcelain cat? I stared intently.

Nothing. I shifted my position to get a better view.

"Where have you gone?" I said in a sing-song voice.

Tilting my head, I still couldn't see it. I tried another angle. It seemed okay. Perhaps I had scared it away? Relaxing just a bit, I leaned forward.

Suddenly the cat flew towards me with an evil hiss. It vaulted over the other cats in a giant leap, easily clearing its porcelain brothers and instantly covering the distance between us. Its claws were out as it attacked me with a maniacal show of force. I turned my face to keep the claws away. I threw my arm up and tried to lean back. I felt like a dreamer fighting some creature in a nightmare. The cat's sharp claws caught my 'I heart Tokyo' shirt but didn't penetrate the armor underneath. Thank heavens for the armor.

With its claws caught in my shirt, the cat snapped its yellow fangs at my face. Its mouth was a dark hole. Up this close it was much larger than I had imagined. On me, it seemed less like a cat and more like a panther. Had it increased in size? The other porcelain cats weren't this big or this heavy. The weight of the cat on me caused me to stumble backwards. I fell, tripping backwards over a small difference in height of the floor. Kicking wildly, I managed to get it off of me, and I struggled to regain my footing.

The cat/panther fell back and away from me. It hissed again and then crouched down for another attack. I braced myself. I wanted to keep my unprotected face away from its savage claws.

Just as the cat came flying towards me I caught a glimpse of a sword in my peripheral vision. Ken had come back for me. His sword was out of its scabbard. He gripped the handle of his steel blade tightly. I chanced a quick glance at him. He had the same grim look on his face that I saw when he got into fights at school. He was all focus and determination.

The creature leapt towards me, and as it did Ken's sword swept around. It made a broad arc and connected with the cat/panther just above its shoulder. The creature shrieked, but it wasn't the sound of a cat. It sounded almost human, a savage scream of pain and anger. Making an angry hiss, it disappeared behind a counter in the shop. Ken followed it around the corner of the glass display case, his sword in his hand.

"Be careful," I shouted. The cat/panther was gone. It had disappeared somewhere, possibly ducking into the back of the shop. Ken returned to my side, looking around cautiously.

"What was that thing?" Ken asked as he inserted the blade's tip into the waiting mouth of his scabbard. He was panting, and his eyes were wide with surprise.

"I don't know. One minute it was a porcelain cat sitting in the window. The next minute it was clawing at me," I said, feeling the blood draining from my face.

Kanbei and Katsushiro came up quickly behind Ken. They had been a step ahead of Ken and immediately returned when they noticed we weren't there.

"Are you okay?" Kanbei asked full of concern for my harrowed condition.

"What was that thing?" I repeated Ken's question, a little too loudly in order to hear it over my own beating heart.

"*Maneki-neko*," Katsushiro replied. His voice was calm and greatly reassuring, but I noticed his hand stayed on the hilt of his sword. I could see he still gripped it tightly.

"I thought those were just ceramics. Little glass things you put up in the window..." I sputtered.

"Mmm..." Kanbei said, continuing to search the room for any sign of danger.

"They feed on people's greed," Katsushiro explained, now focused on me with an intent look on his face.

"Greed?" I asked trying to catch my breath. This was the second time that day that I felt the adrenaline pumping through my veins.

"Yes."

"Whose greed?"

"Perhaps the greed of the shopkeeper. Perhaps the greed of those who come here."

I struggled to understand. It didn't make sense to me. I'd never seen anything like this before. How could I have missed something like this?

"Are they all like that?" I finally asked.

"Not all. Some," Kanbei said.

"They are becoming stronger," Katsushiro added gravely.

"Don't people notice them? I mean I think I would notice a panther moving through my store."

"Again, it is the Blindness. People don't see it."

"How can they miss a panther?" I asked.

"They don't see what their own greed is doing."

I shuddered when I thought about that thing skulking around some shopkeeper's store, while the humans around it were ignorant of the danger. Worse yet, the beast grew stronger with each passing moment, feeding on the greed in its environment. This thought set off in me another fit of hyperventilation, and I struggled to control it.

Meanwhile Kanbei was eyeing Ken the way I imagine a potter looks at clay. Having returned just in time to see Ken's skill with the sword, he seemed impressed. I wondered if Ken's skill with the sword had come as a surprise.

"That was good work," he said clapping Ken on the shoulder.

Ken beamed, soaking up the good-natured praise from Kanbei. We had known him for only a morning, but I could tell he wasn't the sort of person who would offer compliments without a reason.

"Did I kill it?" Ken asked optimistically.

"These kind are hard to kill," Kanbei said, shaking his head. "But you have scared it off."

If Ken was disappointed, he didn't show it. For a moment Kanbei smiled. Then, as if remembering something, he was the serious samurai again and the smile vanished from his face.

"We should keep moving," he ordered us, and we headed out of the store down the road towards the Palace.

When we left the store, I was more careful to keep together with the others. It was strange for me to think of Tokyo as a dangerous place. It had been, up until today, the safest place we had ever lived. There was little crime, and the city was easy for us to get around. How odd to think that I wasn't safe here. First, I had encountered that terrible blue *oni*. My mind flashed on the incredible strength of that awful creature. I had felt so powerless in its evil grip. And now the wicked *maneki-neko*. I stared at my ripped t-shirt and imagined the damage that it would have done if I had not been wearing armor. Two savage events in the same day. What would they say at school? How would I ever explain it to anyone? Who would believe me?

I looked over at Ken. He was adapting to the reality of our new normal without a problem. He held his sheathed sword in his hand and chatted with Katsushiro who was teaching him the names of the sword parts in Japanese. *Saya*, the scabbard. *Tsuba*, the guard. *Tsuka*, the handle. Ken was absorbing the details, repeating them with more confidence.

"This is unlike any Japanese lesson we've ever had," I thought.

The temperature was dropping, and I could not see the sun. The morning had seemed so promising, but now heavy grey clouds crept into the sky, choking off what little warmth was left of the day. The air was getting colder, and I rubbed my hands together, cherishing the last remnants of my body's heat. The wind was like a cold slap on my face, but as we walked together I felt warmer.

Kanbei walked next to me, observing the people on the sidewalk who paid us little notice in return. He was taller than I was and had no trouble setting the pace. I moved quickly to keep up with him. Moving along in silence, I wondered how to put my feeling into words. In a matter of hours everything that I knew about my life and the world we live in had changed dramatically. Now I found myself caught up with two men dressed in samurai clothes, marching to an unknown destination. The threat of death by blue Japanese troll was hanging over my head.

I said nothing, but Kanbei seemed to intuit what I was thinking. He was like that. Always observing, he was able to sense my feelings sometimes before I knew what I was thinking myself.

"It is a lot to absorb all at one time," he said to me, his tone gentle and reassuring. I imagined this is how you would talk to a nervous horse. I was the horse.

"Yeah, I'm not sure how to feel," I confessed.

"It is perfectly normal to have a mixture of feelings," he said.

I wondered how many people Kanbei had initiated into his world of killer *oni* and attacking porcelain cats. Had others fared better than me? Ken seemed to be making the adjustment without a problem. I turned to glance at him walking with Katsushiro a step or two behind us.

"I don't know how I am ever going to explain this to my father."

"The important thing now is your safety."

I nodded silently.  I was thinking about what Dad would say if he could see Ken and me in our samurai outfits.  I knew he would be worried about us.  I was worried about us too. At least we had the samurai to protect us.

"Have you always been a samurai?" I asked after a long pause.

He looked surprised at the question.

"No," he answered after a moment. "But I think it was always my...calling."

I enjoyed watching Kanbei choose his words.  He spoke with precision.  Although English was not his first language, his accent was not like the Japanese people I had met before.  I wondered where he had learned it.  How long had he studied? As we walked together I watched him carefully.  He grew aware of my attention and scratched his head shyly.  I was surprised at the thought of this powerful samurai being shy.

"Who do you guys work for?  Are you a club?" I asked after a bit.  My mind raced with questions, but I wasn't sure how much I should ask.  Perhaps I was already asking too much.  Prying. I felt awkward asking, and I bit my lip and laughed a bit so Kanbei would know he didn't have to answer the question if he didn't want to.

Kanbei laughed.   "Yes, I guess you could say we are a 'club'.  We serve the Emperor.  We exist to serve him."

"Oh, you mean the guy on TV?" I asked.  The Emperor appeared on the news in Tokyo.  Not frequently but enough so that I might recognize him if we ever met.

"No," Kanbei said laughing again.  "That fellow is an actor. He is uh...uh..." Unable to come up with the word himself, he turned and asked a question in Japanese to Katsushiro who was a few steps behind us.  I didn't understand the question, but I caught one word in Katsushiro's reply.   It was "stand-in". Katsushiro's English was more idiomatic than Kanbei's, and he had a bigger vocabulary.

"Ah, yes. That's it," Kanbei said in English to me. "The fellow on TV is like a *stand-in* for the true Emperor," he said, emphasizing it the way one does when learning a new word.

I weighed this answer for a moment, wondering why the Emperor would need a stunt double.  I doubted the answer would be something I would want to hear. I changed my line of questioning.

"Well, what is he like? The true Emperor?" I asked Kanbei. Hearing us talk of the Emperor, Katsushiro joined the conversation.

"The Emperor? He is amazing. Unlike any..." Katsushiro's voice trailed off.

"It is too hard for me to describe," Kanbei said in agreement. "Just to be in his presence changes a person forever."

I looked at Kanbei not knowing what question to ask next. He glanced at me, and as if reading my thoughts, he continued.

"It is as if every cell in my body suddenly knew what I am here on earth to do. Just kneeling in his presence, I knew that I was meant to be a samurai. As if it was always meant to be, but until that moment I had never fully understood it. He kindled a burning passion in my heart."

I wondered what kind of person could cause such a profound reaction in a person. In just a few hours I had found such admiration for Kanbei. He seemed so strong. So confident. Now to hear him talk about the Emperor in such glowing terms made me wonder what kind of person the Emperor must be to command such respect.

"Tell me about the *oni*," I asked Kanbei.

"*Oni*?" his countenance changed immediately.

"Kanbei-san does not like to talk about the *oni*," Katsushiro explained to me. "Their evil is too great."

"I want to know," I said firmly. No one said anything for half a minute.

"The *oni* are an abomination, a horrible blight on our land," the older samurai finally said with a sigh.

"They seem so powerful," I said feeling the fear well up inside of me again.

"They are," Katsushiro told me. "They kill whatever they want. They are like wolves among sheep."

Kanbei frowned at him. I could tell he did not want the younger samurai to frighten me. Finally, he said, "It is true that few dare to oppose the *oni*. Their evil is ancient. No one knows how they originally awoke in Japan. Perhaps they were always here, created by Ame-no-minaka-nushi for the benefit of man."

"Ame-no-minaka-nushi?"

"Ame-no-minaka-nushi," Kanbei said, looking at me as if I had just asked him "Why is there air?"

"Oh, *that* Ame-no-minaka-nushi," I said nodding my head as if I understood.

Kanbei must have seen the look on my face and explained, "The great God in the Center of Heaven. He is the greatest of all the deities – the one who existed before all the other deities and lives in the center of the Ninth Heaven."

I nodded again, and Kanbei continued, "Or perhaps the *oni* were the product of some early sin of man. Who knows what shapeless dormant evil took form in these dreadful creatures?"

"Unlike the other *yokai*, the history of the *oni* is obscure," Katsushiro interjected.

"*Yokai?*"

"What you would call monsters," Katsushiro explained. "*Yokai* tales are like ghost tales. Stories of the strange, the fantastic. Supernatural monsters."

"We do know that the *oni* were not always as evil as they are today. In the past there were times when *oni* and humans lived in close proximity."

"Humans lived close to *oni?*" I could not believe it.

Katsushiro answered, "There is a saying: *oni mo minareta ga yoshi*. It means even an *oni* is good looking if you get used to looking at him."

Kanbei looked at Katsushiro without any expression on his face for a long moment, but then turning to me, he went on, "But the blue *oni* have always had a desire for unholy things."

"And a penchant for eating human flesh," Katsushiro added, apparently sharing what he thought to be the most important part of the story. Kanbei shot him a warning glance.

"At any rate, they proved too dreadful to be in close proximity to humankind. They were cast out of contact. In their solitude, free from all redemptive influences, the monsters' evil compounded. They defiled themselves and became an abomination."

"How horrible," I said quietly, thinking about the *oni* that had tried to kill me.

"Yes, and their power is becoming stronger," Kanbei went on.

"Very few are left who can oppose them," Katsushiro added.

"Has anyone ever beat the *oni?*" Ken asked.

"Once. Six centuries ago. At that time the *oni* were almost wiped out," Kanbei said.

"What happened?"

Kanbei paused for a moment, took a deep breath and then told us this story.

*"Six centuries ago, in the era of Bunmei, there was a young samurai named Momoyama Taro in the service of Hatakeyama Yoshimune, the Lord of Noto. Taro was a native of Echizen, but at an early age had been taken as a servant by the daimyo of Noto. He had been educated under supervision of that prince and instructed in our fighting arts. As he grew up, Takeda Taro proved himself to be a good student. He learned quickly, was patient and had a pleasant personality. He was admired and much liked by his samurai comrades and all who were in service to Lord Yoshimune.*

*"One day when Momoyama Taro was about 20 years old, he was called into service by Hosokawa Masamoto, the great Daimyo of Kyoto. Under orders from Lord Masamoto, Taro sought to drive the oni out of the land. A great battle ensued. Many lives were lost and many brave deeds were done, but the bravest among them was Taro. After a long period of fighting, the humans won. Finally, the oni scourge had been driven from the land. Only a few oni remained and the ones that survived fled to a small island off the coast. Momoyama Taro thought to follow them and exterminate them forever as Lord Masamoto had ordered. He and his men pursued them as far the coast, but for whatever reason he did not put an end to the oni. His men begged him to follow the oni to the island, but he refused. Some say he was bewitched. Others believe he entered into some unholy alliance with the oni. Or perhaps he just lost his will to fight on. But for whatever reason he did not pursue the surviving oni. All the oni that we face now are descended from those that Taro failed to dispatch.*

A peculiar quality hung in the air now, as if Kanbei's story had opened some communication with the past that pressed in on us. The air had a heaviness to it. We walked on in silence for a moment, but I couldn't help feeling an unpleasantness. It was odd to think that my current problems could be traced to that one moment in time and the actions – or rather the inaction – of one man. As for the samurai, I got the feeling they believed collectively they had failed me.

Finally, Katsushiro broke the silence. "Without opposition the *oni's* power only grows."

"The blue *oni* are pure hatred. Pure hatred in animal form," Kanbei said gravely. "They become stronger while we wait for the bravery of another samurai."

Suddenly and quite without warning, a terrible feeling took hold of me. I had not felt anything like it before. It felt like death. Maybe it was that Kanbei's story had acted as some incantation, invoking Taro's ghost, but I was suddenly gripped by the feeling that I was going to die – like a funeral in my brain. I could actually feel the dread creeping up my limbs. The blood seeped out of my face, and my legs weakened. A terrible sensation grew in the pit of my stomach, making every nerve feel numb. My arm throbbed in pain.

"This can't be happening," I muttered quietly to myself. "What have I done?" A terrible sense of regret overwhelmed me as I walked along with the samurai. I longed to go back to another time before the attack. Why had we gone into that shrine?

"No. No. This can't be happening," I said under my breath. "This can't be happening to me."

We fell silent and continued on together, hoping to walk out of the odd ominous feeling that had overcome us. Lost in my dark thoughts, I inched closer to Ken. The samurai were a step behind us, intent on keeping a close eye on us now. Their presence comforted me, and I let my mind wander to the events of the day. It had begun so simply and then turned so dreadful. I thought for a moment about the blue *oni* and shuddered. I could feel the hair on my arms stand on end.

"It's out there," I told Ken. "I know it. I can feel it." To reassure myself I looked over my shoulder at Kanbei and the handsome Katsushiro walking behind us. We had just met them, but already I had come to trust them. They had risked their lives for us.

I wondered though if they could protect me from the monster. Would I ever be safe? The blue *oni* could be anywhere, lurking in the shadows. It could be just ahead, waiting for me. The thought made me uneasy. We continued walking.

Ken's eyes hadn't left me and after a while he broke the silence.

"So, Maya?"

"Yeah?"

"Can I ask you a question?"

"That is a question," I answered, instinctively teasing him. It felt good to fall into a comfortable place. Razzing my brother came naturally to me.

"Yeah, yeah, yeah," he shot back without missing a beat.

"So?" I asked.

"What were you going to get me for Christmas?"

I laughed. I had forgotten the task that had pulled us out of the house that morning. Leave it to Ken to find a way to lighten the mood. We marched on but now in better spirits.

About that time, we came to a place where the pedestrian crowds thinned out. Looking ahead, I noticed a large wall close to the sidewalk in front of us. It was constructed in a Japanese style, plastered in a dull yellow and topped with ancient-looking brown tile. My first thought on seeing it was that it looked out of place among the modern buildings on Aoyama-dori which we had just passed. Rough and imposing, it was easily twice my height, and I could not see over the top.

To say that the wall aroused my curiosity is an understatement. Almost from the moment I saw it, I began to wonder how long it had been there. And equally interesting to me was this question: what was on the other side? An unusual urgency filled me. Immediately, that feeling eclipsed all my other thought, and it did so with an intensity that was stronger than anything I had felt before. It was an urgent desire to know which suddenly welled up in my belly.

"Oh, look at this!" I said, looking for Ken and pointing to the wall. With smug self-confidence, I stood there with my arm outstretched, gesturing towards the wall. I knew for a fact that whatever was on the other side would be the most amazing thing imaginable. I told Ken with certainty that this would be better than anything we'd seen so far.

He nodded his head. Or maybe he didn't. The truth is I didn't notice. I was focused only on the wall and whatever was on the other side.

Pause. Now why was I suddenly so interested in what was behind that wall? I remember a flicker of hesitation crossed my mind, but this was immediately chased away by intense curiosity. All rational thought took a backseat to my feelings.

Looking back, I realize I should have stopped to think about it all more carefully. What was compelling me so strongly? Of course, now it's easy to dismiss my impetuousness, and with the benefit of hindsight, it's clear that I was getting carried away. However, at the time a strange dark desire overwhelmed me. More than anything else, I longed to walk through the entrance and to see what was in there. Whatever it was, I knew it would be interesting, and for that instant, the impulse was too hard to resist. It tugged at my mind, drawing me in.

I had the vague notion that Ken who was standing beside me said, "Cool!" Or something like that. He was focused on the entrance too, and when I looked his way, I seem to remember a peculiar expression on his face.

"Let's check it out," I called to Ken, already stepping forward and not really waiting for his response. My mind was now made up.

"Uh, maybe we should just keep going," I heard Katsushiro cautioning us from behind. I was surprised when he spoke, as if I had forgotten he was there. Glancing back, I saw the two samurai had stopped at the entrance, either unwilling or unable to follow us into the courtyard.

"Now that's odd," I thought momentarily, observing the two over my shoulder as they hovered near the entryway. Katsushiro had the same look on his face that my biology teacher had when my lab partner accidentally dropped the guts of the frog we were dissecting all over the tests that we had just finished and awaited grading.

"Why aren't they coming with us?" I wondered briefly but didn't stop to think about it more than a moment.

Something on the other side of the wall had begun to call to me, and I could hear it inside my head. It was a soft voice at first. Was it singing? It had a melody, almost like a song. Such a sweet sound. Like some top ten song played on heavy rotation on the radio, it was catchy, and I couldn't get it out of my head.

Still, I couldn't shake the concern that our samurai guards were not coming with us. It had been such a comfort to be with them, and now their absence nagged at me.

"Maybe we shouldn't," I started to say, more for my own benefit than for Ken's, but my curiosity – that feeling that whatever was on the other side of the wall was going to be wonderful – got the better of me.

Before we knew it, Ken and I were through the gate in the wall. The moment we entered, the air inside the garden felt warmer. A lazy haze floated by, giving the place a dream-like quality. The warmth was a relief from the brisk air along the street. Someone had been burning incense, and the smell was sweet and thick in the air.

Behind me I heard Kanbei say something, but his voice was distant and hard to make out, as if he were in a car with the windows rolled up. Although we had only gone a few short paces, the samurai seemed far off. And, of course, there was that singing again. Not knowing if it was real or just in my head, I couldn't help thinking I had heard it somewhere before. The melody seemed so familiar. Oh, what was it? I knew if I concentrated on it I could remember.

"Those samurai aren't really important anyway," I heard myself think. What? My own thought surprised me. Did I really believe that? It was such a strange notion. They were the ones who had kept us safe until now. I thought for a moment about the respect that I had felt for Kanbei just a moment ago. Hadn't I just been musing on how much these two had done for me in such a short span of time? Then my thoughts drifted off. I couldn't concentrate, and I let my concern slip away.

"Whatever is in this walled courtyard is what really matters to me," I thought. Why were we following those samurai anyway? They didn't seem like much fun. I tried to remember why we were together, but there was that lilting sound in my head. (What was that tune? It still escaped me.) How had I met those samurai anyway? The events of the morning seemed fuzzy. It seemed like such a long time ago, as if the hazy air was changing my perspective.

Music coming from further inside the walled compound drifted out to me with the smell of the incense, and the singing in my head matched the music. It was the experience I had had before at the mall when I'm humming a tune in my head and then enter a store to find the same song playing on the radio. As if the outside world was playing the music in my head.

"Oh, that it so..." he searched for the right word. "Nice," he finally said dreamily, echoing my thoughts exactly.

Ken and I wandered together through a small gate in the wall which gave way to a stone walkway. Great flat stones the size of manhole covers wound through carefully trimmed plants which grew on either side of the pathway. The beauty of the place overwhelmed me.

"What a cute little garden," I said.

Delighted by the adventurous feel of it, Ken and I walked excitedly along the pathway. Pink camellia flowers grew on a dark green bush beside the walkway. They were so beautiful. I couldn't take my eyes off of them. The dark green leaves were lush and thick with poky edges. I thought I might prick my finger on one if I tried to touch it. The flowers were an exquisite pink. The stamens were bright yellow and impossibly delicate.

Looking at the flowers, my spirits soared. I couldn't remember ever being this happy. Surely this was the most incredible place in the world. Why had we never visited before? All that awful business in the shrine seemed so long ago, if I remembered it at all.

The air was thick and full of incense. It wafted through the garden from some unseen source. For a moment I felt a choking sensation as if it was too thick to breathe, but I made up my mind to inhale deeply and swallow the sweetened smoke into my lungs. With that, I was able to relax into the feeling of the place.

Now Ken was just a step ahead of me on the path. He turned to look at me, and all I could do was smile. He beamed back at me through the thick incense. I don't think I had ever appreciated how very handsome Ken was. For a moment his face reminded me of our parents, but that image of them slowly receded into the distance like an old photograph fading with age before your eyes.

I glanced down from Ken's face to the walkway that circled around from our location to a courtyard a short way off. Drifting forward, my brother and I entered the courtyard and encountered hundreds of...foxes. They were real foxes. *Kitsune* in Japanese. Young and old. Grey and red. Foxes of every size and color suddenly swirled around us. Lithe bodies contorted on little black paws, bristle brush whiskers shot out from white muzzles, and everywhere frantic tails swished in the air together.

The sight of all those *kitsune* together in one place was memorable enough, but the thing that most remains in my memory is the sound. The *kitsune* made the strangest noise. It wasn't at all like a dog's bark. It was high pitched and reminded me of a yodel. The sound of the *kitsune* barking their strange little cries and jumping over and around each other is an indelible image burned in my brain.

"How can there could be so many foxes living in the middle of Tokyo?" I asked Ken.

"It seems odd, doesn't it?"

"What are they doing here?" I asked him, but of course he didn't know either.

"Surely someone would notice this many foxes," I said half to myself, but I was in such a great mood and we had already seen so many strange things that day that I was prepared to suspend my disbelief. I wondered who would take care of them. They seemed so friendly. So adorable.

During this time, I had absolutely no worry or fear. It never occurred to me that the *kitsune* would hurt me or try to bite. There were so many of them – well over 100, although there was no way to count them because they were moving around so quickly. They could easily have overwhelmed us if they had wanted, but I knew that they wouldn't. Bright and animated, they were unmistakably amiable.

While I was still wondering who could possibly look after so many foxes, I gradually became aware that music was louder here in the courtyard. They lyrical sound immediately made my spirits soar. Ken laughed. I heard his voice through the thick air. The huge contingent of foxes surrounded both of us and followed us as we walked slowly. Their little black feet jumped over one another in a swirling mass of fur and ears and tails all around us. I was trying hard to not step on any white tail tips that swished around me.

"This is wonderful," I said, and when I spoke the foxes danced with excitement. My words sent a shimmer out through the sea of fur surrounding me, like ripples in a pond. As if my words themselves were animating the *kitsune*.

"Isn't this the best thing ever?" Ken replied and the foxes reacted to his voice too. They shimmered, shaking their coats and wagging their tails even more furiously with each word.

Something about the foxes made me so happy. Their merriment was contagious. I was so caught up in the excitement that I did a little skip. Immediately the foxes around me reacted joyfully, jumping and swirling in response to my movement. It was almost as if they were delighted I was dancing. I pawed my hands in the air, making a gesture that I thought looked like a fox. The *kitsune* squealed in glee.

Do it again, they seemed to say. Or did I imagine that? There was that singing again.

"Ken, look what I can do!" I shouted to Ken, thinking to teach him but he had already learned the trick. He was doing an amazing impression of a fox and the foxes around him squealed in delight.

"Do that one again!" This time I clearly heard one say. It was one of the foxes. He was speaking to me in a high fox voice.

"Do this one with your paws," another fox called out to Ken and did a little prance. Ken made the same motion with his hands and sending a ripple of delight through the foxes. It was applause for his efforts.

"Again. Again. Again," they all shouted.

"Now do this with your tail," one called out. Ken obliged them by swishing his tail.

Wow. That's odd. "I didn't know Ken had a tail," I said out loud. One of the foxes standing close to me shouted above the din, "You should use your tail too."

"Oh, I don't have a tail..." I started to say, but when I looked behind me and saw that in fact I did have a tail, I let my words trail off and gave my own tail a swish. It gave me such a wonderful tingling sensation. It was extreme sensory stimulation, sending a ripple up my spine and into my brain. I loved the feeling.

At first it was a complete surprise to me that I suddenly would have grown a fox tail. I swished my tail again. A moment later it didn't seem so strange. I swished it again. In another moment, it had become like the most normal thing in the world. Swish. It was as if I had always had the tail. I began to flick it back and forth with total abandon, and the foxes around me jumped up and down and laughed in delight. I admired my tail's red fur and its white tip. Every swish sent an amazing sensation through my spinal cord and straight into my brain, lighting up a place in my brain I'd never experienced before.

"What a wonderful thing!" I called out. The foxes around me squealed in delight, reacting to every word I said.

"Yes! Yes!" they shouted. I was becoming a fox too. Becoming one of them. Had these foxes been human once too? I wondered for an instant, but a moment later the thought was gone, banished from my brain by the intoxicating singing of the *kitsune,* the delightful feeling of my own tail, and the strong thick smell of incense hanging heavy in the air.

All this time I was touched by such an overwhelming feeling of belonging. The little foxes were so excited to see me. It was as if they had always been expecting Ken and me and they were so happy to welcome us. It was something like the feeling of coming home to family but a hundred times more intense.

I couldn't help but laugh. I looked over at Ken. Where had he gone? All I saw was a happy posse of foxes singing the most pleasant melody and rolling together on the ground. They frisked together and jumped. They were a sea of motion.

"Ken?" I called out. I had to show him my delightful new tail.

"Let's play some more," called one of the foxes I was dancing with. I started to dance for a moment but could not lose the image of my brother.

"Where is Ken?" I asked. For a moment – it was just an instant really—I saw Dad's worried face and thought what it would be like to tell him I had lost Ken. For just an instant the smile vanished from my face.

"Ken?" I called again. This time more urgently. Where could he be?

"Let's forget about Ken," shouted one fox above the din of the others.

"The day is young. Let's dance some more," the *kitsune* closest to me breathed the words heavily in my ear and wagged its bushy tail. The fox pulled at me. From his words I could tell he badly wanted me to forget my brother. It was so tempting. Maybe I could stay for one more dance. No, but it just seemed...wrong. And why was this fox so insistent? Where had Ken gone? As good as I felt, I couldn't shake the notion that something was wrong. My conscience troubled me.

"No! I have to find Ken." When I yelled the *kitsune* danced back away from me. There was a small circle around me. For just a moment my head cleared. Ken was my brother. I remembered that much. I couldn't just leave him. And this... this was wrong. I could feel it for just a moment. I tried to cling to that feeling.

Again, I saw my father's face. He looked so worried. He was trying to say something. It was like a dream. I knew he was talking, but I couldn't make out what he was saying.

All around me it was choruses of "Come play! Come play!" The swirling tangle of foxes was so tempting. Every word they said rang in my head, like a catchy melody that you can't shake. The joy of dancing with them was so appealing. I knew, though, that I had to focus on doing the right thing.

"No, this isn't what I am here for," I shouted this time a tad angry that the foxes were not helping me find my brother. The little creatures fell back further.

"Ken?!" I yelled. The fox squeak had left my voice. I felt more human and the tingly sensation that ran up my spine subsided.

Suddenly I heard a response.

"I'm here."

It was Ken's voice. I could hear him above the voices of the foxes that were still singing the melody.

"Ken?" I looked around for him. The *kitsune* continued to part around me, making space for me to walk.

"Maya! I'm here." I could see my brother now. He was coming toward me. He still had a fox's tail and whiskers protruded from his face, but he was starting to look human again.

"Ken, we have to get out of here," I said. My words sounded more urgent than I actually felt.

"I think you are right." As Ken said the words I felt incredibly sad. It would be such a pity to leave the bewitching company of the *kitsune*. Seeing that Ken was safe, my resolve waivered. I hesitated. I thought 'Maybe just one more dance before we go.' I desperately wanted to spend more time with the foxes.

I saw again a vision of my father. He interrupted the swirl of foxes around me. His lips were moving. What was he saying? I could tell from his expression that it was very important.

"What is it? What are you trying to say to me?" I wondered. I couldn't hear him. I tried to focus. He looked so sad, repeating the same thing again and again. In my mind, I watched his lips. I finally got it. I finally understood what he was saying.

"Maya, run!" he said urgently. It was like someone had just turned the volume of the TV up. It brought me out of the dreamlike stupor. Like being splashed with cold water. I knew he was right.

Ken must have seen it too. "C'mon, Maya," he said. He grabbed my hand.

I made up my mind to leave and turned around. Immediately, Ken and I were alone. The foxes had disappeared. Rows of stone foxes lined the path we were on, but the furry playful creatures were nowhere to be seen. Everything was immediately quiet. The music had stopped. The stone foxes watched us from their stone pillars. Silent. Frozen. Something about the foxes had brought us joy. But now that joy was gone.

Something in my heart felt sadder than I had ever felt before. I thought I was going to cry. Turning to look at my brother, I saw Ken's face looked just as glum. We began to leave.

"What just happened? That was so odd," I glanced at Ken who looked like he was struggling to choke back the tears. "What had been so tempting about the foxes?"

"Now I just feel...guilty," Ken said, shrugging.

We were human again. There was no trace of the fox tail that I had a moment ago, but the feeling of having the tail was still there. I felt a tingling sensation, and I could still feel in my head the joy of swishing it, even though it was gone.

We walked along the stone path back to the gate in silence. The pink camellia flowers along the path were no longer as vibrant, as if the color had been washed out. The air was still thick and full of incense, but it was no longer a welcome smell. Instead, it was smoky and bugged my eyes.

Our samurai friends Kanbei and Katsushiro paced in front of the entrance to the courtyard we were in. They had not entered. They said nothing but were looking at the ground.

"Kanbei?" I said. He looked up, but he was embarrassed. He would not look me in the eye. I knew that it was for me. Did they know what had happened to us? Or perhaps they had seen us? Watched us transformed into foxes? Although it felt as if we had gone deep into the garden, it might not have been far away at all. Perhaps they had seen everything.

I trusted the samurai, but it surprised me at the time that they had not come to our rescue. Of course, I had no way of knowing the truth – that they never would have entered the courtyard to save us. Their heart for discipline never would have allowed it. Had we not returned, they would have abandoned us to the *kitsune*, and we would have remained there with the others, trapped in the garden transformed into foxes. They had done all that they could do, which was to watch us from the entrance and wonder if we would ever return.

"I thought..." Katsushiro started, but Kanbei cut him off with a small gesture of his hand that made Katsushiro stop immediately. He was about to say something about the *kitsune* courtyard, but his voice trailed off.

"There is no reason to speak of this again," said Kanbei. His words had a finality to them that weighed heavy on my heart. Later I came to believe that he spoke out of graciousness. He said it for my sake.

The minute the words were out of his mouth, my shame was overwhelming. I knew I had done something wrong. I could feel my conscience tugging at me. I felt the first tear run down my cheek, which I tried to hide from Kanbei and Katsushiro. I hated to cry in front of people, and I didn't want them to see me. I turned my face away. I felt so bad about what had happened, but I didn't know how to put it into words.

Ken was quiet too as he picked up the sword he had dropped at the entrance. He stuffed it back into his belt. We walked out through the gate and started down the road again in silence. We went slowly, not talking. I looked at my shoes as we moved, my tears burning my cheeks. We had passed the samurai's test, but just barely.

Chapter Four
Visiting the Imperial Palace

We followed Aoyama-dori towards the Hanzomon gate of the Imperial Palace. The street was broad, wide and – like every other street I had ever been on in Tokyo – immaculately clean.

I recognized the area, of course. Aoyama was the posh part of Tokyo, full of stylish salons, spas and pricey smoothies that would make your skin look ten years younger. It was further subdivided into two areas: north and south. Aoyama-dori, on which we now walked, connected Kita-Aoyama with its more refined sister, Minami-Aoyama, to the south. I suppose Kita-Aoyama was just as well-to-do as Minami-Aoyama, but in Kita-Aoyama you were more likely to find a little old Japanese lady emerging from her narrow apartment to sweep the sidewalk in front of her home.

I had been to the area on some errand or another since moving to Tokyo, and I recognized the address as belonging to several of the "beautiful people" at school. I didn't *know* them, of course. I knew *of* them. And knew that they lived here. I found myself making the same snap judgments about people who lived in Aoyama as I had about people who lived in Beverly Hills when we were in LA. Perhaps the comparison was appropriate. Aoyama was one of Tokyo's oldest suburbs, originally the domain of Tadanori Aoyama, an early and highly trusted vassal to the first shogun of Japan. Of course, at that time it had all been green fields and streams. Now, even though it was covered in concrete, it had an ocean-like quality to it. Waves of people and cars washed over the pavement. To me it was the one stretch of road in Tokyo that was never congested with traffic.

Cars zoomed by us as we walked along the wide sidewalk. For a moment I let myself imagine the comfort of sitting in a taxi. Until that day, taxis in Tokyo had always been a pleasure. Unlike our experiences in some of the other cities where we had lived, I had always found Tokyo's taxis to be clean: white lace seat covers, drivers in elegant white gloves and doors that opened for you automatically. How comfortable it would be to sit in one of those now.

My fantasy of traveling comfortably in a clean taxi was abruptly interrupted when my imagination inserted a terrible blue *oni* into my daydream. Suddenly, I saw its blue body running with incredible speed alongside our taxi and smashing through the window with a massive taloned hand. In my mind's eye it reached through the shattered glass of the window. Its hand was dirty, gravedigger dirty. The sharp talons were just inches from me. I had to get away. I scrambled across the taxi's seat to move as far away from the monster as possible, but I couldn't get away. The hand kept coming. With no place to run, I pushed against the far door of the taxi trying to kick the sharp talons away, but it was useless. In my vision, I opened my mouth to scream, but no words came out.

I shuddered, trying to rid the thought from my mind. The images in my head were becoming more realistic and harder to shake. My imagination was working overtime now. Visions of the monster were increasingly appearing in my thoughts and taking over my memories.

"You're not real," I told the monster. "Get a grip. It's all in your head."

I willed myself to think of something else.

Turning to the samurai who had tried to save me, I focused on them. I focused on their clothes, on the hilt of their swords. I thought of anything that would try to ground me in the here and now. I had enjoyed Kanbei and Katsushiro's protection so far, but even with the reassurance that their samurai swords gave me, I did not feel completely safe.

"They are going to help me," I repeated over and over like a mantra, but some part of my brain didn't believe it. The image of the horrible blue *oni* returned. Every time I closed my eyes, the monster was there waiting for me. I was unable to shake it.

The fact that I didn't understand what was happening to me only made matters worse. I had trouble processing it. The *oni's* poison was working its way through my body, contaminating my brain, wrapping a chokehold around my neurons. The stress of the situation had accelerated my decline. My life had gone from the "normal" setting to "extreme danger" in just one day. My mind was on high alert, but my body was tired from a dreadful sense of fear.

I tried – I really tried – to push the evil thoughts out of my mind, but despite my attempts to think of something positive, the image of the terrible *oni* kept creeping up on me. Would the *oni* come back to eat me? I tried not to think about the prospect of becoming a Happy Meal for a blue *oni*, but my mind wouldn't let me escape.

Unintentionally, I replayed the events of the morning. I sort of let my guard down and suddenly I saw myself in the shrine in slow motion. It had an immediate physical effect on me. As I thought of the terrible creature, I could feel the blood seeping out of my face. My legs felt weak and my arm began to throb. A sense of dread crept up in the pit of my stomach, making my body feel numb. A wave of nausea came over me, and I had to fight the urge to vomit.

"When we get there, it will all be okay," I thought, looking forward to the safety of the Palace and the Palace guard. Katsushiro had assured me that the guards of the Imperial Palace would welcome us and help us to get to the Kabuki-za theater. I wasn't sure what kind of help we could expect from the people there – Kanbei had called them magicians – but I was ready to do anything if it would keep us away from the terrible blue monster.

Just when I felt I had my mind back in control, something would set me off again. Touching the tear in my sleeve, I tried to remember if the *oni* had licked me before or after the tear was made. It was no use. I couldn't remember, but touching my sleeve triggered some weird kind of memory. I sniffed the air. Then sniffed again. Suddenly, the stink of the monster's breath filled my nostrils. It was like a flashback in smell. That set me off again, making my stomach clench.

I was an overwound jack-in-the-box, tense and afraid something would happen at any moment. They say that people with a phobia of some sort or another have the same kind of irrational fear. It was inescapable.

The worst part was the loneliness I felt. "What have I done?" Blaming myself, I felt an incredible desire to go back in time. If only I could go back to my life before these terrible things had happened. "I'll need to leave Japan. My family will never be safe around me again." If I was being pursued by that terrible monster, I couldn't be around Dad and Ken. It wouldn't be safe for them. I imagined a life without them. How lonely would I become? "This can't be happening." I remember thinking. It was a feeling of such regret.

I wanted it to just go away, but whenever I tried to push the thoughts out of my head, evil crept back in and took hold of me. Like bugs under my skin, it was an irrational feeling that I couldn't escape. I took a thin breath, feeling long and drawn out.

"Maya? Maya?" It was Katsushiro. His voice was gentle, but it startled me. I had forgotten that others were there. It was as if I had already started traveling alone.

"Yes?" I said in the tiniest of voices. My stomach muscles were tight as I tried not to be sick. I held my breath. The fear was so strong in me that my body began to shake.

"We are almost there," he said pointing at the black gate of the Palace. Something about his manner calmed me and brought me back from the edge.

"Maya," Katsushiro said again. He was looking at me carefully. I knew he understood what I was thinking. He gripped my arm, gently but firmly. It was a warm wonderful feeling.

"I am not alone," I told myself. He was close to me now, standing beside me. His eyes were studying me, but I didn't sense him judging me. I knew he understood my predicament. I tried to relax, tried to force myself to breathe. My nose flared as I sucked in air.

"We are almost there," he said again, holding on to my arm. He was an anchor, pulling me back to reality. After a moment, I nodded.

"Okay," I said. "I'm okay."

Katsushiro studied me carefully, trying to decide if he could believe me.

"What?" I said, pretending to be more exasperated than I actually felt. "I said I'm okay. Really." I quickened my pace to show him I was alright, as if a demonstration of walking speed would emphasize my point.

The days were short in December, and it was early evening when we arrived at the Palace. The imposing black gate to the Palace was huge and quite a distance from the road.

"Cool," Ken said almost under his breath as we got closer.

"What is that?" I asked, pointing to what a looked like a large pond.

"That is the moat which circles the Palace," Katsushiro explained, still eyeing me carefully.

"First time here?" Katsushiro asked Ken.

Ken nodded.

"Yeah, me too." I volunteered.

"Maya, you'll be safe here," he added after a moment.

I nodded, not sure if I believed him. I wanted to believe him. I wanted to know it would be okay.

The samurai conversed with each other in Japanese. Then, sensing my nervousness, Kanbei spoke up, "Maya, the moats and walls of the Palace have protected it for centuries. You *will* be safe here."

The traditional Japanese architecture of the Palace stood in contrast to the modern city around it. Behind us was the busy intersection, and I could still hear the sound of car tires on asphalt coming from it. Ahead of us, a gravel path led to an enormous wooden gate which had a small roof with blue tile covering it. Small pine trees, pruned to be just a little taller than a man's head, stood sentry on the gravel walk to the gate. It was carefully cultivated. Immaculate.

We walked along the gravel toward the gate, until a guard dressed in a grey uniform appeared and intercepted us. Supposing us to be tourists, he made an anxious hand motion for us to stop. The Palace was not open to tourists. Then he apparently recognized Kanbei and Katsushiro. His posture abruptly changed, and with a refreshed attitude, he motioned for us to approach. Approaching the guard, our samurai spoke quickly in hushed voices. After conversing with the samurai for a minute or two, the guard looked over his shoulder nervously, his eyes darting back and forth. I wondered if they were telling him about the blue *oni*. The samurai gestured towards us as they spoke, but I couldn't make out what they were saying.

Standing next to me, Ken rubbed his hands together. The sun's light was fading and the temperature was dropping again. Walking quickly in our armor had kept us warm during the day, but now that twilight was here, I was getting colder. The grey sky to the East made me think it was going to snow. It was certainly cold enough now.

"Do you think that guy is one of them?" Ken asked me, interrupting me from my thoughts about the cold. We were a short distance from the samurai and the guard.

I shrugged. It was hard to think of samurai in anything but their samurai attire.

"I guess he could be. Think he's still a samurai despite his clothes?"

"I wonder how many of them there are."

I stared carefully at the guard and his uniform. Squinting at him, I was confident that he really was wearing modern clothes, and it wasn't just my eyes playing tricks on me. What had Kanbei called it? The Blindness? It wasn't the Blindness that was making me think that way.

The guard turned to open the gate and Kanbei called to us.

"Ken, Maya...come this way." He gestured for us to follow him.

As we passed through the gate, the guard bowed deeply. Ken and I tried to keep walking after our samurai guards and bow at the same time with limited success.

Just as we crossed the moat and entered the Palace grounds, I thought I saw snow. I looked up. The clouds were thick to the East, but the sky above us was clear. Little snowflakes reluctantly materialized out of nowhere and then quickly disappeared again. Appearing for an instant in front of my eyes, the flakes vanished when they landed on the ground. The ones that fell on my clothes lasted longer. I looked down at the snow on my sleeves.

"Run away, little snowflake," I thought. "It isn't safe for you here." In a moment, the snow stopped.

Ken and I followed the samurai down a narrow gravel path lined on each side by shoulder-high pine trees towards an immense black gate which loomed in front of us, impressive and unyielding.

This was Hanzomon Gate. It was the only entrance in a very high wall which ran from left to right as far as I could see. Easily three times my height, it had a rough-hewn stone base with a smooth white plastered wall built on top of that. A sloping roof of grey tiles adorned the top of the structure, while immaculately manicured pine trees were scattered along the wall in both directions.

The trees blocked my view for the most part, but off to one side I could still see a bit of the inner moat that surrounded the Palace. The still water in the moat reflected the image of the Palace in the fading light of the day. It was quiet and still – and felt utterly at odds with my emotional state.

From inside, I heard a noise and slowly the massive black gate opened with a creaking sound, heavy wood groaning on ancient hinges. A second guard, interrupted from some Palace task, pushed it open from the inside. Entering the gate, we stepped out of the chaos of Tokyo streets and into the tranquility of the Palace grounds.

I had been expecting a castle or some modern building, but from our vantage point all I could see was trees. It was as if we had stepped into some forgotten woods. Japanese feudal woods. Behind me I could still hear the faint buzz of traffic, but when the guard pushed the gate closed behind us, the sound stopped as if the spigot had been shut off. From the woods in front of me, I heard a bird chirping.

We walked for some ways through the woods behind our guard who led us over along a gravel path towards a squat wooden building. It was a single-story structure almost totally eclipsed by the trees around it. A sea of grey rocks surrounded the base which gave me the impression that the building was floating. I couldn't tell if it was a trick of the shadows caused by the small veranda or if the building was actually floating. The entire structure was quite small and didn't seem very impressive, although the traditional Japanese architecture and that strange floating illusion made the building stand out in my mind. Certainly not something I had expected inside the walls of the Imperial Palace.

"This is the Palace?" I muttered to Ken. From the outside, the room didn't seem much larger than my bedroom at home. "What could be in this tiny space?"

"Hmmm," Ken replied noncommittally. He craned his head around, carefully studying the building and our surroundings. If anything, he was reluctant to judge too quickly based on appearances. Ken was quicker to adjust in that way than I was.

In front of us, the samurai opened a sliding door in the wooden building so we could enter, and I saw a staircase descending into a much larger room below. In fact, there wasn't much more to the room we were in than the staircase down and a small wooden bench. I eyed the bench suspiciously. It looked quite delicately made.

"Please wait here," said Kanbei politely, gesturing towards the bench. He and Katsushiro disappeared down the wooden stairs leaving us standing in the entryway of the small room.

The minute Kanbei and Katsushiro left the room, panic gripped me. They had left us alone. I shot a glance at Ken. He seemed unconcerned. I could tell. He looked around, curious about his surroundings, while I scanned the trees outside for any blue threat. It was the first time the samurai had left us on our own since the attack, and the soothing effect the Palace grounds had on me was immediately overcome by a growing sense of dread.

"Wonder where that goes?" Ken said aloud as he tried to peer down over the edge to see where the stairs were leading. They disappeared into darkness.

I didn't have an answer. I was busy looking to see if anything was trying to sneak up on us.

"Maybe we should follow them," he tried again, pointing towards the stairwell with his chin.

"They told us to wait here so that is exactly what we are going to do."

"It's just that —" he started, but I cut him off before he could finish.

"Look, you don't know what kind of place this is. There could be danger anywhere. The last thing we should do is wander off from where we were told to wait. We should just sit here until they come back to get us. So stop talking about wandering around the Imperial Palace and sit down."

The room sunk into stony silence. Ken lost interest in the dark stairs and fidgeted on the bench kicking his shoes into the ground. Convinced I had made the right decision, I examined the room with renewed interest.

From the transom above the doorway, a carved wooden dragon looked down at me from a swirling mass of heavy grey clouds. The carving was so skillfully done that the clouds appeared to roll across the back of the dragon, swelling then ebbing in wave after wave until they rolled off of the transom.

The samurai had left the sliding door of the little room open, and from that opening a weak winter light filtered in and lingered on one side of the dragon's face. In the dim light I couldn't be sure, but I thought the clouds were actually moving through the sky.

As I stared, the dragon locked eyes with me from its position. Angry eyes in dark sockets stared down at me. I gulped, wondering if the dragon was about to fly out of the carving at me.

Remembering my experience with the *maneki-neko*, I adjusted my sword. The weapon itself made me uncomfortable, and I would not have drawn it from its scabbard. But I was thinking about how I would run from the room and the sword was an encumbrance I would have to deal with.

I was about to mention the dragon to Ken, but before I could do so, we were joined by another samurai. He did not come up the stairs that Kanbei and Katsushiro had used but abruptly appeared behind us.

He wore the same *kimono* as our friends and had two swords stuck in his belt. The border of his *kimono* was stitched roughly – I could see the handiwork – and he wore it turned up around his neck like a high collar. His hair was pulled back in a ponytail, exposing his face which was gaunt and angular. His broad square forehead supported by bushy eyebrows. We stood to our feet when he approached us and when we did, he bowed courteously. We tried to bow in return without much success. Formal Japanese etiquette was not my strength at the time. The corners of his mouth twitched, but he did not smile.

"My name is Kyuzo," he said, his face not moving.

"It is nice to meet you. I'm Maya."

"I'm Ken."

The samurai grunted, then bowed again slightly. His manner was cool, with an intensity of focus that reminded me of Kanbei and Katsushiro. Unlike those two, however, I felt a distance with Kyuzo. I could not imagine myself sharing a joke with him the way I did with Katsushiro – or even with Kanbei for that matter. He was too serious for that. Honestly, from the moment I met him, I found him to be intimidating and sensed in him a capacity for violence lurking beneath the surface.

I guessed his age to be between that of Katsushiro and Kanbei. I was sure Katsushiro was a teenager or maybe a little older, not much older than me. I imagined Kanbei to be in his sixties, but it was hard to tell. He had moved with such athleticism in the park. It was hard to think of him as "old" in the conventional sense. I peered down the stairwell, wondering where the two had gone and when they would return.

"They will be back with you in a moment," Kyuzo explained, noticing the direction of my gaze. His words had the effect of focusing my attention back in the room. He stared openly at our *katana*, our swords, while I squirmed. There was something about his penetrating stare that made me uncomfortable.

*"Naka naka ii katana desune,"* he said, then corrected himself into English: "Those are quite nice *katana* that you have there." His tone was serious as he inspected the weapons we had been carrying around since we bought them at the used clothes store in Omote-Sando. Something about the way that he said it made me want to take a step back and put my hand on the hilt of my sword.

"Do you know how to use them?" he asked. It was amiable enough, but there was something about the way he said it. There was an edge to it. Was it a challenge? He was genuinely interested. I knew, though, that he meant something particular when he asked if we could "use" the swords.

"You bet we do," Ken said with a great deal of confidence, causing Kyuzo to raise an eyebrow.

"We've had some opportunity, but I can't say that we are good at it," I replied, thinking this was a more honest answer.

"Ah, well let's spend a moment to practice." His voice was cool and his expression was flat. It was hard to resist, drawing me in against my better judgment, as if his voice was tugging at me.

Ken glanced at me, and I tried to tell him with my eyes that this was a bad idea. He shrugged and said, "Sure."

"Good. Now come this way," Kyuzo said, and with that he turned on his heel and proceeded down the stairs, Ken trotting after him. I followed reluctantly, worrying that Katsushiro and Kanbei would return to find us gone. We had no way to get in touch with them if we were separated.

"Ken, we have to wait for them to come back," I protested weakly, but I was already unsure if I could I could find my way back. It was our first trip into the elaborate warren of rooms under the Palace, and Kyuzo had brought us through a maze of hallways, down a corridor, and towards a large *tatami* mat room.

"You will have time before they return." Kyuzo brushed my concerns aside as he walked quickly into the room.

Following his lead, we kicked off our shoes and stepped up onto the *tatami* floor, resting our swords by the door. The scent of the fresh mats gave the room a comfortable feeling. They were soft beneath my feet.

The room was sparsely decorated, with paper *shoji* doors on two sides and dark wood paneling on the other two ends of the room. Seven wooden and bamboo swords were mounted on the wall at the far end of the room. The ceiling was surprisingly high, considering that we were in the basement.

At one end of the room, there was a slightly raised platform, like a small stage six inches higher than the rest of the room. This too was covered with *tatami* mats.

"Let's have a cup of tea before we begin," Kyuzo said, pointing to the platform. He sounded polite enough, but it wasn't a request.

I was still cold from our long walk outside, and a cup of warm tea sounded very nice right now. Following Kyuzo's gesture, we took our places on blue cushions loosely arranged around a small table on the platform.

Immediately one of the paper-thin doors slid open and a young boy, maybe a little younger than Ken, brought in a tray with the tea. He must have been waiting for us on the other side of the thin door, patiently listening for Kyuzo's cue. He was dressed in a light grey *kimono* and a thick black *obi* belt that covered all of his slender body from his navel to his rib cage. He looked like a miniature version of our samurai escorts. He had big expressive eyes and glanced at Kyuzo with a cautious look on his face. Setting the tray on the table in front of us, he backed up, bowed, and silently exited the room.

I remembered my conversation with Kanbei and wondered how long Kanbei had been a samurai. Had he joined when he was as young as this boy? I wished we could have talked to the boy before he left. I was eager to know what it was like to be a samurai living here, but something in Kyuzo's manner made it hard to ask these questions. I wished Katsushiro would return.

"Please," said Kyuzo gesturing towards the tea. Ken and I reached for our tea. The tea "cup" was large...almost like a small bowl. Inside it, the tea was hot dark frothy and green. I took a whiff. It smelled pungent and I was worried it was going to be awful. Kyuzo was right there. How would I avoid drinking it? Then I smelled it again, only to find the odor had changed. This time it was sweet. It made me think of... birthday cake.

"Now that's weird," I thought, taking a small sip. The tea exploded on my taste buds. It was easily the best thing I had ever tasted. It felt like spring had come to my mouth.

"Wow! This is fantastic," I gushed. I looked over at Ken. He was emptying his bowl and eyeing the bottom wistfully. I rolled the bowl in my hands, swirling the last sip of the thick green substance in the bottom. I eyed it carefully, sad that it was over. A moment later it was gone. I stared at the bottom of the bowl, hoping that Kyuzo would notice and call the young boy back to offer us a refill. But no such luck.

As soon as we finished, he sprung up abruptly and motioned for us to do the same. He walked to the paneled wall at one end of the room and plucked two bamboo swords from the wall. Handing them to Ken and me, he returned to the wall and grabbed a third for himself.

The swords were one piece of bamboo but had been split vertically into four long slats. A leather fitting covered the handle and another small leather piece covered the tip. The handle felt good in my hands. It was a bit lighter than my sword. I bobbed the bamboo blade up and down, feeling its balance.

"First things first," Kyuzo said, pulling my attention away from the bamboo sword in my hands.

I wondered what was first. I looked to Kyuzo but he just returned my gaze with a stern expression on his face. Since he didn't tell us we began to guess.

"The correct grip of the sword?" Ken asked tentatively.

"No," he said.

"A formal bow?" I guessed.

"No," he replied.

Ken and I looked and each other and shook our heads. We were out of ideas. I shrugged.

"First take off jackets," Kyuzo said.

Kyuzo took off the cloak that he wore over his *kimono* and Ken and I took off the sweatshirts and the t-shirts we had bought at the store in Omote-Sando. My t-shirt was badly ripped from the *maneki-neko*. We waited for his orders in our armor.

"This is a *shinai*," he said, gesturing to the bamboo swords that he had given us. "Good for practice."

As he spoke, my mind felt fuzzy. "The long walk has left me sleepy," I explained to myself. It felt like I had just gotten up from a long nap. Feeling a little queasy, I noticed I was wobbly on my feet. Trying to take stock of myself, I stared at the bamboo sword in my hands.

"What had he called this again?" I was thinking to myself, struggling to remember the word. And then — as if someone had just turned the light on in a dark room – the fuzzy feeling fell away. Everything clicked into place. I could see everything, as if scales had fallen from my eyes. The world was so clear and my mind was unbelievably alert.

"It's a *shinai*," I answered my own question, not meaning to speak aloud.

"Yes," Kyuzo agreed. He studied me carefully.

I looked at Ken. It was just a quick glance, but in that instant, I saw so much. It was an abundance of detail. I saw that he had the slightest trace of green foamy tea still on his lip. I saw that his armor had come undone beneath his left arm. I noticed most of his weight was on his rear leg. Most importantly, I saw that he had the same intense look on his face that I knew I must have. He was looking at me, and in that moment – it was really just a millisecond – I knew that he had sized me up in the same way.

My mind was working at a 1000 miles-per-hour. I was absorbing everything in the room, every minute detail of Ken and Kyuzo, the feel of the *tatami* beneath my feet. My first thought was that nothing escaped me, but the more I saw in the room, the more I realized there was detail yet to see.

Before I could put anything into words, Kyuzo called us forward and taught us how to use our *katana*. The lesson was underway before we knew it.

Immediately, Kyuzo's movements changed as well. He moved with remarkable smoothness. He looked like – water. His graceful motions made me remember our samurai friends in the shrine that morning. Everything flowed. There were no wasted movements.

Kyuzo would show us a move and then we would repeat it. He would position our hands and then let us move. Sometimes he would stop us and correct us, physically repositioning our bodies and correcting our motions. At other times he would instruct us. His remarks were always positive, always encouraging. But he never smiled.

"Good! Keep your elbows closer to your body."

"Don't swing so wide."

"Excellent. Do that again."

Ken and I began to sweat. Our feet moved awkwardly on the *tatami* at first but more confidently as time went by. Kyuzo never offered us a moment of rest. That strange "lights on" feeling in my head continued. What had been in that tea? I could intuit

Ken's moves. I became aware of the smallest things. His left foot twitched before he did a downward strike...time to block above. His grip tightened before his strikes...a moment to prepare. I felt a calm come over me. For a moment it was as if I had always held this sword. The *shinai* sword became an extension of me. Ken seemed to be feeling the same way. His swings became faster and his thrusts more accurate. He blocked my counter attacks and quickly moved to a new position.

"Good!" Kyuzo said after we had been practicing for what felt like hours. "The energy flows through your hands...through your hearts...through your minds."

My bangs were wet with sweat from the exertion.

"Now let's try two against one," Kyuzo ordered. "You two attack me."

Ken and I immediately turned to face our teacher with our *shinai*. Without saying a word, Ken and I split apart so that we could attack from opposite sides. Ken stepped to the left, and I moved to the right. How did we know to do that? It was as if I could read Ken's mind. I couldn't hear his thoughts of course, but I could see the minutiae of his behavior and know what he wanted. It was all in the details. In my heightened state I noticed the smallest of things, and knowing Ken, I could easily interpret what the details meant. Looking at the way his balance shifted ever so slightly from his front foot to his back foot, I knew that he wanted me to attack first.

Taking the lead, I thrust the *shinai* at Kyuzo. He parried my strike and immediately swung his bamboo sword around at me. I just barely managed to block. The moment he was committed to his strike at me, Ken launched his attack. I could see that Ken's timing was perfect. His *shinai* came whizzing through the air straight at Kyuzo's head. I thought for sure he would land his blow but Kyuzo shifted his weight, moved his head and the sword went flying past him narrowly missing his face. I saw that Kyuzo's movement had shifted his balance and saw my opportunity. I struck again. Then Ken again. Our moves were perfectly timed with one another. If I was reading Ken's mind, then he was reading mine as well.

For a moment I thought of Kanbei and Katsushiro as they had fought the *oni*. Their moves had been this way, perfectly in tune with one another.

The *oni*. I had almost forgotten. The thought of the blue monster hunting for me made my heart freeze. My mind was racing, and I imagined how I would fight the *oni* now. Gripping my sword tightly, I wondered if I would be able to swing it at the monster. The speed with which my mind was working only made the image more horrible. The terror became more real, and I imagined every detail of the encounter. I wondered if I could even pull the *katana* out from its scabbard. Would I be willing to use it? I hated the thought, believing it to be useless. The monster was more powerful than I could imagine, and it would easily overwhelm me.

"There is no way I can win," I thought in desperation, and the awful image of that blue evil eating me swept through my mind.

Suddenly I felt the loud thwack of Kyuzo's *shinai* connecting with my arm. It brought me back to reality.

"Ouch..." I complained.

"Don't be lost in worry about the future," Kyuzo instructed as if reading my mind. "Just think about the present." Could he tell that my mind had been wandering? I looked at him and saw that he was studying me carefully.

Just then one of the sliding *shoji* doors opened, and Kanbei and Katsushiro came back into the room. They were walking with another samurai who was talking rapidly in Japanese.

I was breathing hard and focused on the red welt emerging on my arm. It would not be the last time I would walk away from a practice session bruised and bloodied. Once, I broke a thumb when a training sword connected with it, but that was early on, and each time I learned from my mistakes. Despite the pain on this occasion, I felt a huge sense of relief wash over me when I saw the two samurai return.

"How did they do?" Kanbei asked Kyuzo in English for our benefit, an expectant look on his face. His eyes were earnest and I could see that he was anxious to know how we had performed.

"Well," Kyuzo said, without any trace of a smile. "Remarkably well."

Ken beamed. Kyuzo was the type of person who would not say one word of compliment beyond what he intended. I tried to make a polite bow but ended up feeling stiff and awkward.

The samurai who came in with Kanbei and Katsushiro was named Takeshi I learned later. I didn't take note of it at the time but no one introduced us to Takeshi. Until that time everyone had been careful to introduce themselves and allowed us to introduce ourselves to them. It had been a reciprocal show of politeness.

But not with Takeshi. He was a general and exuded confidence even among samurai like Kanbei and Kyuzo. He was one of twelve *hatamoto* generals and reported directly to the Emperor himself.

Takeshi looked at us the way our school bus driver had looked at Ken when my brother had eaten too many carrots and barfed on the bus floor that day. I wondered if he could have heard about the incident with the foxes. I felt ashamed again momentarily, and I'm sure I blushed, but Kanbei had said that there was no need to speak of it again. I had known him for less than 24 hours, but I could tell he was a man of his word. He would not have said anything, and I did not believe he would have told General Takeshi about our failure.

I wondered if Takeshi was less cordial than the others because we were putting his men in danger. Perhaps he was concerned because his men were now fighting to protect us. I thought of the danger that Kanbei and Katsushiro had exposed themselves to by taking us on. This seemed a more likely reason for his chilly demeanor.

After hearing the report of our swordsmanship, all of the samurai immediately started speaking to each other in Japanese.

"What do you think they are saying?" I whispered to Ken.

"I think Kyuzo is telling them there is absolutely no way we are ready to fight an *oni*," Ken replied.

I laughed.

"Yeah, but you were looking pretty good out there on the mat, Ken."

I had been genuinely impressed with how proficient he had become while we practiced. How had we become so good so quickly? How long had we been practicing? It felt as if we had been on the mat for ages.

"You weren't so bad yourself," he shot back. I allowed the corners of my mouth to go up in smile.

"It feels like we were out there forever," I said. "As if time had stopped and the only thing that existed..."

"...was sword fighting," Ken said, completing my sentence. Something had happened to us while we were out on the mats. Ken felt the same way.

"The tea?" I asked.

"That's what I was thinking," he said. His mind was racing with the same speed that mine was. We were both hyper-attuned to every detail in the room.

"Learning tea?" I asked.

"Could be," he replied.

"We were moving the way they moved," I reflected.

"The samurai at the shrine?" Ken said it as a question, but he knew immediately what I meant.

"When they were fighting the *oni*," I added.

"I was thinking that as well."

We both turned to look at the samurai now discussing our fate. Katsushiro, Kyuzo and Kanbei stood in front of Takeshi with their heads slightly bowed, staring at the floor. Their hands were at their sides. Takeshi was speaking in a harsh tone of voice to the three, who occasionally responded to his questions with one answer or another.

"I suppose they are trying to decide who is going to take us to the Kabuki-za," I guessed, nodding towards them.

"Probably the low man on the totem pole," Ken offered.

"Not quite," Takeshi said suddenly switching back to English. He had been listening to us. "All three of them will accompany you to Kabuki-za," he said coolly.

The three samurai said "*ha*", yes, and bowed in unison again.

"Kanbei!" Takeshi continued.

"*Ha!*" Kanbei said, still bent at the waist in his bow.

"Let them rest here for a moment, feed them, and then get to Kabuki-za as quickly as possible," he instructed our escort.

"Yes sir," Kanbei said in English to his master, still looking down at the ground in his bow.

"And you two," Takeshi turned his attention towards us, causing my heart to freeze. "Obey your escorts. If you fail to obey them, you might not live long enough to regret it."

Ken and I said, "yes sir" and tried unsuccessfully to improve our bows. Takeshi looked at us out of the corner of his eye with what I took for open contempt. He turned on his heal and strode quietly out of the training room.

The minute he was out of the room, I breathed a long sigh of relief and wondered if I had been inadvertently holding my breath. It was my first exposure to the strict hierarchy of the samurai.

"I did not like that guy at all," I whispered to Ken who nodded in response.

We followed Kanbei to the next room. There was a small wooden box on the floor. It was the size of the small TV in my room at home. Inside the box was a metal lining, and inside the metal lining were several small pieces of charcoal. A kettle sat on the fire and steam rose from it. Beside the little stove was a tray with rice wrapped in some sort of leaf. I suddenly realized how hungry I had become. When had we last eaten? All of us sat down around the stove and Katsushiro passed out the rice balls. I unwrapped the leaf and took a bite of the rice. It was the best food I had ever eaten.

"The tea accelerates the mind," Kanbei explained to us without being asked. "Makes you more mindful of the lesson. Helps you to retain the information longer. What you learned here will not be easily forgotten."

"It was an amazing feeling," I said between greedy mouthfuls of rice.

"Like someone turned on the lights," Ken added, his mouth full.

"You felt that way too?" I asked my brother. He nodded, taking another huge bite.

"It is a unique feeling," Kanbei agreed. "And less dizzying after time."

I wondered what it would be like to practice in this heightened state day after day. (I also thought about the grades I could get.)

"It also increases your caloric requirements," Kanbei explained. "Be sure to eat." He offered us the plate, and both Ken and I happily helped ourselves to a second helping. The rice was amazing.

Ken ran his finger along the handle of his sword, examining the grip. I could see by the look on his face that he was still in the heightened state, his mind accelerated by the tea. He fingered the silk cord that wrapped the handle of his sword, counting the diamond patterns in it.

Kanbei watched him intently.

"It's so beautiful. So well crafted," Ken said.

After a moment, Kanbei said, "The sword is one of humanity's finest killing tools, but for us it is a way to attain inner peace."

He paused for us to absorb what he was saying

"Interesting, isn't it? That a weapon of war could become an instrument of peace?"

"Peace," I repeated. It felt so far away. "I don't think I could find peace right now." I felt overwhelmed with the thought of blue *oni* trying to devour me. I knew if I closed my eyes the awful images would return.

I looked hopefully at the empty plate but was sad to see nothing left there. When we were finished, we reluctantly got up to leave.

"How long will it take us to walk to Kabuki-za?" Ken asked.

"We will travel underground in the safety of the Palace until *Seimon*, the Main Gate, and then it is a short walk from there," Kanbei informed us. "Thirty minutes."

Kanbei had been right. The Palace had been a safe place for me, and it had been refreshing to not worry about the *oni*. Well, not worry as much as I had before we arrived. But now we were headed back outside the Palace walls, and my mind immediately began to spin. I could feel the tension creeping back into my shoulders. Despite the fear, or maybe because of it, I was eager to get to Kabuki-za. If there was a chance that the people there could help me get out of my predicament, I wanted to find it.

Chapter Five
A Night Out at Kabuki-za

The walk to Kabuki-za was quite pleasant despite the cold temperature. Our route to the theater had us edging closer to the Sumida River and the bay and the wind was colder here. It had the ocean's edge to it now. But the snow had stopped – at least for the moment –and I felt refreshed and warmed after our time in the Palace.

Although it was dark and quite deserted in the area around the imperial grounds, we soon made it to Ginza and found many people out and about there. Ritzy fashion boutiques lined the main streets tempting fashionable shoppers, and the neon lights chased away the cold and gave me some comfort.

Ginza was an area of right angles. Broad boulevards alternated with narrow alleys, all laid out in perpendicular fashion, creating rigid blocks in a grid pattern. The curb formed a perfect right angle with the street. And then again from curb to sidewalk. And finally, from sidewalk to building front. It was a model of 90-degree precision and order. But while the buildings conveyed a sense of order, the shops inside them did not. The conformity of the structures could not contain the infinite variety of Tokyo life, and the first floors of these narrow buildings overflowed with a jumble of shops, stores and galleries.

The shops were a hodgepodge of mom-and-pop stores alternating with the flagship stores of every high-end brand imaginable. A fifth-generation traditional Japanese candy maker was sandwiched between Prada and Starbucks. A 300-year-old department store jockeyed with the Apple Store for shoppers' attention.

Heaped on top of these retail venues was another five or six floors of office space. Small businesses of every type squeezed into microscopic quarters, brimming with Japanese office workers sitting shoulder to shoulder. Having completed their work for the day, these people now spilled onto the streets to eat a meal or meet with friends or start the long commute home.

The sight of the hustle and bustle of people made me think of my abandoned errand of Christmas shopping. In my present condition, Christmas was a luxury I couldn't afford, and I wondered if I'd ever get the chance to celebrate again.

These thoughts were on my mind as we passed a brightly-lit department store window. I tilted my head up to take in the building. I recognized it immediately.

Somewhere on my desk at home, I had a postcard of this building. The hand-tinted postcard showed the building with an odd little clock tower above it. An electric trolley, the forerunner of the country's subway system, clattered through crowded streets. I had purchased the antique card at a flea market which we had visited with my father when an old friend from New Haven was in town. It gave me a curious feeling of nostalgia for a Japan I would never know.

Now the trolleys were gone and the people passing by wore modern clothes. Well, except for us, of course. In our *kimono* and Edo era armor, we might have stepped out of the postcard.

Looking up I could still see the clock tower on the old building, peeking out over the top. I dropped my gaze to the first floor of the department store.

The tastefully lit display in the window featured designer bags cleverly arranged in the shape of a reindeer. Wallets made up its legs, a handbag was the shoulder of the deer and a key-ring was its eye. A genuine set of antlers were perched on its head. The key-ring, which was a bit too round and a bit too big, gave the reindeer something of a panicked look as he paused mid-flight in front of a bright red cushion. I saw the reason for his concern. Behind the deer was a handbag bear, its eyes focused intently on the deer. The bear had a gaping coin purse for a mouth and claws made of belt straps which reached malevolently for the deer.

I shuddered. It was too close for comfort.

"Focus on something else quick!" I told myself and then caught sight of our group in the reflection on the window. The three samurai in front, *katana* protruding from their belts. Ken and I together. I had ditched the "I heart Tokyo" shirt at the Palace.

The decidedly military nature of our party was unmistakable. We were marching through the streets heavily armed.

"Isn't it weird that no one looks at us," Ken said at that exact moment. I supposed he saw me eyeing our reflection in the mirror.

"No one stares."

"Kanbei said the world is blind to the reality of it all."

I nodded. Then, after a moment, the oddity of the thought left my mind. I guess dressing like a samurai was becoming normal for me. Here I was in full battle regalia – reluctantly carrying a sword – on my way to meet actor/magicians who may or may not be able to help me in my predicament. Oh yeah. And I was being pursued by blue *oni*. Perfect. Hashtag my new normal.

Moving along together in high spirits, Ken and I excitedly told Kanbei and Katsushiro about our sword-fighting lesson. They listened intently and asked questions about our experiences. Kyuzo looked straight ahead as he walked, listening stoically to our excited retelling of what he had taught us. We covered the distance quickly and after a short time we found ourselves in front of Kabuki-za.

The building itself was magical. Dramatic lights flooded its four-stories, which rose from the street in the middle of Ginza. Bright red banners plunged down the length of the building, announcing a coming attraction – or so I guessed. The banners were in *kanji* and a cursive style *kanji* to boot which was particularly tough to decipher.

The shape of the building reminded me of a castle and was capped with twin gables at the top. The roof was covered in blue shingles. A graceful arch undulated over the entrance like a flowing wave and hanging beneath the arch was a giant purple cloth. The sides of the cloth were drawn upwards on the left and the right, tied with a tassel. It reminded me of a curtain being drawn up to reveal a dramatic production.

A kabuki play must have just finished because a large crowd was milling in front of the building, jockeying for space with the throngs of shoppers wandering the streets. Traditional kabuki plays were long. A four-hour play was not unusual. I looked at the faces of the theater-goers to see if they looked tired or not. It was a mix of foreigners of every nationality and Japanese theater aficionados.  Everyone was chatting with his or her companion, sharing a carefree happiness that felt foreign to me now.

I came up next to Kanbei who scratched his head pensively and surveyed the crowd.  Was he wondering whether they had enjoyed the play or not?

"What's he looking for?" I asked Katsushiro who appeared at my side.

"He is searching the crowd for any sign of a threat."

"Are we safe here?" I asked nervously, looking around for any blue signs of danger.

"Kanbei has a third eye for danger," Katsushiro assured me. In futures years, I would learn what it was like to see the world with five eyes: my two and his three.  But at that moment, my only concern was for my own safety.

"You said that *oni* hate crowds." I meant it as a question but Katsushiro just nodded.  I wondered how safe Kanbei judged this location to be.

Kyuzo took up a position apart from us where he could observe both us and the crowd.   The muscles in my neck tensed.  Judging from his serious look, I'd have guessed that something was terribly wrong, but then remembering that Kyuzo always wore that expression, I relaxed and turned my attention away.

Feeling a momentary surge of relief when we finally arrived at the theater, I cautioned myself against getting my hopes up.  But who was I kidding?  I desperately wanted a solution.  I hoped that our samurai guides were correct in thinking the people here could help me.  My hopes were definitely up.  Way up.

We went down a small alleyway around the side of the Kabuki-za building.  On the side of the building there was a small door, and we entered there.  Even Ken had to duck his head in order to pass through.

"You said the Kabuki actors were magicians," I asked Kanbei as we walked.

"Yes.  Although I am not sure if that is the right word."

"Do they cast spells on people?"

"No, not that kind of thing," he paused before going on.  I wondered if he was considering how much to tell me.  Earlier, I had wondered if he was hesitant to tell us because he didn't want to worry us.  Now I thought perhaps he didn't elaborate because he didn't think I was ready for it.

After a moment, he seemed to finish his mental calculations and went on, "So much of this world is based on what people see. However, as you have already learned, people do not see things as they truly are."

I nodded, thinking I knew what he meant. Indeed, I had seen that to be true. People had clearly not been able to see or accept our samurai outfits as we walked through the streets of Tokyo. I had seen so many things that made me wonder if I could trust what my eyes told me.

"The magicians here have devoted themselves to the art of the unseen. The clues from the universe which we can see point to a much larger universe which we cannot see," Kanbei said.

I nodded again, although this time I wasn't sure I fully understood him.

"That's why we fight, Maya," he went on. "We are fighting for a world we cannot see."

"Do you think they will be able to help me?" I asked finally.

"I don't know, Maya. I hope so."

"Me too." I thought it but didn't say it.

Kanbei's face was serious. He went on: "The actors here inhabit the world of the unseen. Perhaps they can find a solution." He paused as if thinking and then continued, "If nothing else, they will know more about the ways of the blue *oni* than I do. That alone will be helpful."

A guard was sitting in a chair by the door listening to music on an iPod. He watched us with a total lack of interest as we ducked into the room. He wore a grey uniform complete with a tin badge and looked a lot like a security guard at the mall. You know the kind? Not too serious. More worried about catching people littering than stealing. I assumed he was going to take us to someone important within the theater. Then I noticed an odd thing. Perhaps it was the residual effect of the tea that made me notice. It was such a minor detail. The mall-cop had long hair. He was not dressed like a samurai, but I could easily imagine that hair in a top knot like many of the samurai wore.

Privately acting on my hunch, I studied him for a moment. His hands were muscular and I could imagine him holding a *katana*. He had thick wrists. His posture was not rent-a-cop either. He sat leaning to one side almost slouching – but he was completely motionless. Something about it reminded me of a coiled spring.

When we walked in, he switched off the music on the iPod and greeted us perfunctorily in Japanese. *"Konban-wa,"* he said seemingly uninterested, almost to the point of boredom, but his eyes were alert.

Kanbei announced, "We've got business in the theater."

"It's him, isn't it?" I asked before thinking it through carefully. For a moment I believed that the guard was the person we had come to see, but the minute I spoke the words, I was uncertain about my hunch.

"What?" Kanbei asked, looking at me and raising an eyebrow.

"He's the one we've come to see, isn't he? He's one of you," I wondered if I was completely off-base. There was a silent pause. I blushed, feeling I'd been wrong. Had I embarrassed myself?

Then Kanbei smiled.

"Impressive," Kyuzo said, but of course, he didn't smile.

Scratching the stubble on his chin, Kanbei spoke almost to himself, "Appearances can be deceiving."

Then in a voice loud enough for all of us, "Yes, this is the one we have come to see." I wondered for just a moment if Kanbei had been testing me. I had been right. This was our man.

"So, these are the ones I have heard about?" the samurai/mall-cop said in English, grinning broadly. His English was good but not as polished as Kanbei and Katsushiro's. He had a trace of an accent and struggled with his l's and r's.

"Ken, Maya, this is Heihachi," Kanbei said. "He is an old friend and also an authority on all things *oni*."

"You've heard of us?" I asked, curious.

"I have. Your plight is of great concern to us. To all of us. I hope that I can help," he said.

I had the feeling that he had been waiting for us at the entrance.

Heihachi was young. Much younger than Kanbei and Kyuzo. He might have been the same age as Katsushiro, but he had a different way about him. Katsushiro had a purity that made him seem even younger and more handsome – almost beautiful. Heihachi had a mischievous look to him. He was less innocent. Less like a child. I couldn't be sure, but I judged him to be older than Katsushiro.

"Follow me please," Heihachi said and led us into the theater.

Inside, the huge *kabuki* theater was dark and quiet. The lights in the ceiling four stories above us had been dimmed after the crowds had left. Behind me were two stories of balconies, a balcony and above that a second balcony. We had sat in this upper level when my father had brought us months ago. "The cheap seats," he had said at the time, laughing. It had been a wonderful time then in our seats high above the stage. The crowd had brought an energy and excitement to the room, electrifying the atmosphere.

Now the theater was dark and empty. Without the crowd, the theater was quiet, graveyard quiet. I felt like we were trespassing someplace we didn't belong. The small sounds of our footsteps were swallowed up in the lonely hall. Around me, nothing moved. Even the still air was waiting expectantly for the next show.

"Please wait here for just a moment," Heihachi said and then left us alone with a bow.

As my eyes grew accustomed to the darkened room, I realized that people were on the stage.

"Is this some kind of dress rehearsal?" I whispered to Ken. He shrugged, and the theater was quiet again.

The people on stage had emerged without any noise. Or had they been there and I just hadn't seen them? There were two of them, and they knelt side by side, facing us on a small raised wooden dais on the right side of the stage. As my eyes adjusted, I realized they wore grey *kimono* with a large insignia on either shoulder. Some kind of family crest? Each insignia looked like a large creepy eye staring back at me. The two sat in front of a folded metallic screen. I thought perhaps I could see their reflection in the shiny silver screen, but the theater was too dark for that. I saw only murky shadows on it.

The one on the right was a *shamisen* player. He held his instrument, which was shaped like a banjo, resting it in his lap. A slender neck stuck out of the drum-like body of the *shamisen* and three hexagonal ivory pegs anchored three silk strings. It was barely visible in the dim light of the stage. The *shamisen* player had pushed back the sleeve of his *kimono*. In his hand he held a large ivory pick that looked like a putty knife and hovered motionless over the strings.

I studied the *shamisen* player carefully. He was frozen. Oddly frozen. As if he was exempt from time. Then as if coming to life, he began to move – but only his wrist. He used the putty knife pick to pluck one of the strings on his *shamisen*. It was, I thought at the time, the loneliest sound I had ever heard. He plucked another string. *Twang*. The note reverberated throughout the theater, occupying the entire space before dying away and plunging the great hall into silence again. He plucked another note. Then silence. He continued this way. Pluck a string. Pause. Pluck another string. Pause. Slowly the tempo increased.

On the left, his partner knelt quiet and motionless in front of a small podium. Like the *shamisen* player, he too was frozen and expressionless. Large tassels decorated the front of the podium which was built just high enough for someone kneeling. Standing in the theater watching the stage, I couldn't help wondering what purpose this person had. Why was he there with the *shamisen* player? I didn't dare ask the question out loud. As if anticipating my question, the man began to sing. It was a slow mournful song. I didn't understand the words, or course. It was all in Japanese but I knew –somehow I knew – he was talking about a young woman.

The sound of the *shamisen* and the singing resonated with my soul. I'd fallen into a deep pool and was mesmerized by this ethereal world. Enchanted by the strange music and the curious song, I felt myself adrift. Everything else in the theater melted away.

A drum beat abruptly joined the song. I startled. It was a large drum. I scanned the stage for its location. Had I missed it? Was it under the stage? I heard the sound – felt it viscerally—but I could not see the source. A pause. Then the drum again. Slowly, the beat grew in intensity. Faster now, beating at the same erratic pace as my heart. Or was my heart adjusting to the beat of the drum? The tempo increased, carrying my emotions with it.

The two sat there, singing and playing the *shamisen*. I was transfixed. The singer told the sad story of a young noble woman who left everything to be with the one she loved. I can't explain how I knew this. Everything he said was in Japanese, and the way he was pronouncing his words made it extremely difficult for me to understand. Yet somehow when he sang I could clearly see images flash through my mind. A beautiful woman. A house in the snow. A handsome man. The choice she had to make between duty and the feelings that she had for the one she loved. The images came to me through his song, as if he was singing them into being. And yet, so oddly familiar.

The love story was so overwhelmingly sad. The song tapped into a hidden place in my heart, pulling something from me. Dislodging some unexplored memory. Quietly, in the dark of the theater, I felt myself overwhelmed with emotion. I wanted to turn away, but I couldn't take my eyes off the stage. I thought of the loneliness the young woman must have felt. I thought of my own loneliness and my worry that I would have to live life without Dad or Ken. Would I be running from these evil blue monsters forever? I wondered if I'd ever be safe.

Wiping my eyes, I tried to concentrate on the stage. "Don't let them see you cry, Maya," I told myself. Embarrassed, I wiped my eyes. I couldn't understand what was making me so emotional.

Behind the *shamisen* player and the singer, a pale blue curtain hung across the length of the stage. It undulated like water, a wave running across it from one end to the other. I assumed that this meant activity behind the curtain and waited for it to rise. It didn't. Suddenly, seven men behind it pulled it down together. It collapsed on top of them and they ran out together to the left, carrying the curtain with them. I never saw the men, but I could make out their shape beneath it. I wondered what they looked like, but I would never find out.

Behind the curtain, the stage was sparsely decorated. Scraggly branches from a single, leafless tree –I'm sure it was just a prop –hung over the painted backdrop of an icy ocean. The whole thing had the look of a wintry night on a barren beach. It was obviously a stage backdrop on one hand, but at the same time it seemed incredibly realistic. As if the essence of that beach had been boiled down to its most fundamental truth and put up on stage. I felt a cold ocean breeze and shivered involuntarily. It was as if I could actually feel the wind.

The stage was broad. Too broad to see at one time from our position on the floor. I turned left and then right to take it all in. It was dimly lit, but I couldn't find the source of the light. There were no stage lights, no candles, no visible source of that which illuminated the stage. The stage itself had an ethereal twilight glow, as if the sun had set in this theater world and the light from that imaginary star still lingered in the sky. And I was here to watch.

If the lighting was unlike any theater I'd seen before, the shape of the stage was unusual as well. A single thin passage drifted out of the stage to my left, meandering to the back of the theater behind me – presumably through the audience, although there was no one here now. That passage was visible where it joined with the stage in front but melted away into darkness behind me.

Above, the painted sky of the backdrop was total blackness as well. The stage itself appeared to be floating, hanging by some unseen wire. Beneath that inky black darkness, the twilight universe of the stage was frozen, suspended in time, hanging here in the theater.

To my great disappointment, I saw no actors on stage. When the music started, I had hoped we would get a glimpse of a play. Or maybe a practice. But the stage was empty.

Then I saw her out of the corner of my eye. Just outside my field of vision: a solitary woman carrying an umbrella. Her movement caught my attention, and I turned to look. It was the woman from the song earlier. I don't know how I knew this, but I could tell. She appeared from the darkness, walking slowly down the long thin portion of the stage. Had she been there all along?

She walked down the passageway until she was just parallel to us. Heading towards the main stage, she walked in time with the mournful *shamisen* music. The *shamisen* player would pluck his instrument. The woman would take a step. Pluck. Step. Pluck. Step. Slowly she made her way past us towards the main stage. Summoned by the music, she was pulled to the front of the theater by some inexorable power. The music brought her forth, like a ghostly apparition in a musical séance.

Snow began to fall, gently at first then with more intensity, as the woman emerged from the darkness. The snow seemed to fall only on the stage around the woman as if she brought it with her. It fell heavy enough to gather on the ground around her, obscuring her feet. I looked up to see if I could find the source, expecting to see a stage hand hanging from the rafters. It was too dark to see. From my vantage point, the snow seemed to materialize just above the woman. I had seen theatrical snow before and, of course, snow in the movies. If this was the same thing, the effect was completely different. It looked cold and wet. Even from my spot off the stage, I could feel a cold draft coming off its surface.

My attention turned from the snow to the woman. She was wearing a beautiful white *kimono*, covered with intricate patterns. The cloth of the garment shimmered as she walked, adding to the dreamlike effect. The *obi* around her waist was a silver-grey and decorated with a snowflake pattern. From where I was standing, it

89

seemed that the sleeves of her *kimono* were diaphanous, almost see-through, as if she had not completely materialized in this world. It was the most incredible sight.

Above her head she held an umbrella to shield her from the snow. I couldn't see her face. It was hidden by the umbrella. I could make out four kanji characters on the umbrella, but I didn't recognize them. My Japanese at the time wasn't good enough for me to read them. They looked to be hand-painted on the umbrella and seemed to glow with their own light.

With fluid movement she made her way towards the center of the stage, gliding across the floor the way I walk in my own dreams. As she passed me, the umbrella tilted up slowly – just enough to get a glimpse of her face. She was beautiful in an otherworldly way. Jet black hair hung down long, past her shoulders on either side of her face. Her delicate features seemed oddly familiar. Two perfectly shaped lips had a blue tint as did the rest of her skin. I couldn't help but think that I had seen here someplace before. It was almost a supernatural beauty, causing me to gasp almost imperceptibly.

Immediately, she turned and looked right at me. Our eyes met. Hers were entirely black. Black pupils in inky black irises, cold and distant. She held my gaze for a very long time, as if trying to remember who I was. Despite her scary eyes, she wasn't threatening, and I did not feel afraid. Her face betrayed no emotion, but I sensed in her a lingering sadness – like a long drawn-out sigh. Her forward progress frozen while she paused to consider me.

For a moment, time slowed for me, my thoughts piling up like the snow that fell around her. I held my breath for an impossibly long time. Then, slowly, she lowered the umbrella, obstructing my view, as if snuffing out a candle flame. The drum beat continued, and she turned from me and continued to float forward.

When she reached the center of the stage, a young man came out to meet her. He was wearing samurai armor which looked very familiar. It was similar to the ones we wore. He wore white makeup on his face in the style of kabuki actors, but the red accents made his eyes stand out and made him look, I thought, a little bit crazy.

I studied him for a moment before it sank in. At last I recognized him. It was Heihachi, our mall security guard. He must have left us and changed into costume.

Heihachi slowly walked up to the snow-woman, transfixed by her beauty. Almost hypnotized. Like a sleep-walker he approached her, moving in time with the music. It was a beautiful dance the two were performing.

The snow, which fell heavily around the woman, began to encompass Heihachi as well. It fell mostly around her, but as they approached one another it began to swirl and eddy around him as well. I watched the two of them come together. It was like watching a dream.

The sound of the *shamisen* and the singer seemed distant now. While I could still hear them, they seemed far away. Something about the pair in front of me drew me in, blotting out the rest of the theater. We were in our own world and the rest of the theater – the rest of the world – didn't matter anymore. All that mattered was what was on stage.

The snow woman reached out her hand slowly, her delicate fingers tentatively pointing at Heihachi. A pale blue arm stretched out to him. Moving slowly. Pointing to his heart concealed by his armor. For a moment, Heihachi did not react. He waited for her touch, unmoving and mesmerized by her beauty. Then, as if waking up from a sleep, he stepped forward. I thought was going to kiss her hand. Instead he bowed, bending at the waist in a deep formal bow.

Heihachi straightened and pulled something from his belt. It was a scroll, rolled carefully and tied with a blue cord. He gripped it tightly in his armored hand. With solemn dignity, he held it out to her. Slowly extending his arm, Heihachi waited. The snow fell heavily on the scroll in his hands. He bowed again, his arm still outstretched, hand open palm up. It seemed he wanted her to take the scroll from him, as he offered it to her.

Her hand moved towards the scroll. Slowly. Tentatively. As if unsure of what to do. I thought she was about to take it. It seemed that she would, but then she paused, and the two remained frozen like that for what seemed like an eternity.

Suddenly, the woman left. Disappeared. Melting from sight, she vanished completely. I blinked my eyes. What happened? What had I missed? Where did she go? Had she disappeared into some trap door in the floor? Unlikely.

The snow continued for a moment then stopped as mysteriously as it had started. The remaining flakes continued to swirl for a moment on the stage and then were still.

Heihachi remained on stage looking sad. He had the look of one who had just finished a delicious sweet and looks up to find that there is none left. He looked like I felt: close to tears and overcome with emotion.

The curtain fell and the play was over. The *shamisen* music came to an abrupt end. The spell had been broken. I became aware of Ken and the three samurai again. Looking at them, I saw they had been as transfixed as I had. Katsushiro looked shaken. Kyuzo and Kanbei were more reserved, but still visibly moved.

Emerging from behind the curtain, Heihachi motioned to us. We followed him to the opposite side of the theater. He stepped off the stage and joined us on the floor of the theater.

I wanted to bring up the performance we had just seen. I wanted to tell him how moved I had been.

"That was the most beautiful thing I've ever seen," I said breathlessly.

"Thank you, Maya," Heihachi said. "I only wish the ending had been different."

He sighed. I wanted to ask more, but Heihachi moved right into business. Staring right at Ken and me, he jumped into the subject of our recent predicament.

"You are survivors of a blue *oni* attack," he said.

"Just barely," I replied. He was still wearing his stage makeup which fascinated me but gave him a crazy look. I had trouble taking my eyes off of it.

"That puts you in a rather elite group."

"Without Kanbei and Katsushiro, we wouldn't have survived."

"Heihachi, we need your experienced eye," Kanbei said. He wasn't the type to let a compliment hang in the air too long. "Will you help us?"

"Come with me and let's see what we can figure out," Heihachi replied.

Taking us down stairs, Heihachi walked us through a long empty concrete hallway. The green walls were bare, and the florescent lighting buzzed overhead. The sterile atmosphere reminded me of a hospital or a particularly boring school. The floor was shiny, and the samurai's *geta* made a *clack-clack* sound that echoed off the walls as we walked along. At the end of the hallway, an industrial strength door blocked our passage. The metal door matched the flat décor of the room, but the knob was wrong.  It was old –ancient looking really.  Heihachi pulled out a funny shaped key from his pocket, inserted it into the knob, and unlocked the door.

It is hard to describe exactly what happened next. Standing in the hallway looking through the door, I saw a mostly empty room.  There were a few boxes against the wall in the back. It was dark but otherwise perfectly normal.  But when I walked through the door, something very strange happened.  It felt as if I was entering a different kind of air, like that feeling you get when you move from a really cold room to a really hot room.  I'm pretty sure it wasn't the temperature that changed.  It was something else. As if the air itself was actually different.  Something was different. Something shifted. I just couldn't put my finger on what it was.  It was as if there was an electric current in the air.

I blinked a time or two trying to get my eyes to adjust.  I thought it was the difference in the air, but I couldn't be sure. When my eyes were able to focus again I realized that the room was not as empty as I had thought before I walked through the door.  The boxes were still there, but now I noticed that there was also a desk, a screen, and an alcove with a long scroll hanging in it. My first thought was that this was exactly the sort of office I'd expect from a Japanese magician.  It was the kind of room I would have loved to explore at leisure if I hadn't been so anxious to sort out my problem with the lethal blue *oni*.

The far wall – the wall to my left when I entered the room – was entirely made of wood.  It was a single carved surface, painted red.  Perhaps it was lacquered but I couldn't be sure. Carved tree branches – which I guessed to be cherry trees – stretched their branches on the left and the right.  The tree branches were utterly realistic, despite being bright red.  I marveled at the skill of the artist who had made it.  It was a work of art.

In the center of the wall, as if supported by the carved cherry branches, was a carved *mon*, some sort of family crest.  It was similar to the kind of *mon* you find on the sleeve of a *kimono*, but this *mon* was enormous in size.  If I had stood next to the wall and thrown my arms open wide, I would just barely have been able to touch either side of it with my fingertips.  The *mon* was a circle, and within the circle there was a carved flower, a five-petaled cherry blossom.

A scroll hung on the wall in a small alcove.  It was made of rice paper with delicately hand-painted kanji characters on it.  As I stared at the scroll, the characters began to move. First the characters became a bird, morphing into the shape of thrush standing on a reed before my eyes. Then the bird flew away, disappearing from the hanging scroll. An unseen wind blew from the direction the bird had disappeared. The reeds swayed in the breeze eventually becoming two kanji characters again.

At the far end of the room to the right was a folding screen placed in the middle of the floor which blocked my view from the rest of the room. I craned my neck to see what was behind the screen but couldn't get an angle to see.

While I was still taking it all in, the samurai began to talk. Kanbei quickly explained the events of the morning.

"This should be easy enough for them," Heihachi said at one point in the conversation, nodding in our direction. Kanbei scowled at him, and I wondered what he meant by that. They switched to Japanese and took a step towards the screen, away from where Ken and I stood. Their voices dropped to a conspiratorial tone, and I was left to wonder.

I turned my attention to several black and white photographs hanging on the wall above the samurai. Grandfatherly men clad in *kimono* with serious expressions gazed down protectively at the contents of the room.

"What is all this stuff?" I asked my brother, as we waited at Heihachi's desk. Every inch of the desk was covered in a jumble of scrolls, long skinny wooden boxes, and strange implements. It was a crazy mix of science and superstition. "Is this what you'd expect on the desk of a Japanese magician?"

Some of the items were easily identified. I saw a microscope and another thing that I was sure was some sort of telescope.

"Maya, look at this," Ken said, holding what I assumed was the horn from an *oni*. It still had a blue tint to it. I shuddered when I saw it. Feeling queasy and looking away, I told Ken to put it back its place.

"Put it down, Ken! Don't touch that."

A small movement in the corner of the room caught my eye. I hadn't realized it until then, but there in the alcove was a live monkey. It had brown fur and a pinkish face. Sitting on its haunches, it watched us for a moment with wide-eyed stare. Suddenly, it yawned and looked away in that way that some primates do, seemingly to let us know that even if we were a threat, he wasn't worried.

I, on the other hand, was not sure we were friends. Remembering my moment with the *maneki-neko*, I studied the creature carefully for a moment before turning to continue to inspect the room.

Many items seemed familiar but were hard to identify. In one corner was a small globe. Well, I thought it was a globe anyway. It sat on a metallic contraption of gears and chains that I couldn't recognize. The moon was perched on a wire that emerged from the gears. A small crank protruded from the base. I was sure that if I cranked it, the earth would orbit the sun and the moon would move in circles around the earth. Kanji characters decorated the contraption.

I reached out to touch the globe, causing it to wobble slightly as if it was going to fall. The gears shifted with a *clack-clack* noise.

"Nice work," Ken teased me in a whisper. I looked back to the samurai to see if they had noticed.

"It's an orrery," the monkey said. His eyes had been tracking us as we fidgeted at his desk. "A mechanical model of the sun, earth and moon."

"Ken, that monkey can talk."

"Yeah," Ken said, his eyes wide with surprise.

"What's this?" Ken asked the monkey, holding up a shiny silver ball. It looked like Christmas ornament, but had no hook, no apparatus to hang it on anything. It was just a shiny polished ball.

"That's a niobium rotor," the monkey said, providing no further explanation. He yawned again and busied himself with the fur on his left knee.

"Ken, that monkey can talk," I said again still in disbelief.

"All monkeys talk," said the monkey, still fiddling with his knee.

"No, they don't."

"Yes, they do," said the monkey, looking up from his knee with an indignant look on his face. "You've just never heard one before."

Ken and I looked at each other. Neither of us had ever heard of a talking monkey.

Just then, the samurai rejoined us at the desk, switching to English for our benefit. The monkey yawned again and looked away.

"It happened in the middle of the day," Katsushiro was saying.

"Perhaps because of the day?" Heihachi asked.

"The day? Why is this day different than any other day?" Ken asked.

"It is *Ichiyou Raifuku*," Heihachi explained. "The Winter's Solstice. The shortest day of the year."

"What difference does that make?" Ken asked the question that was on my mind.

"It is the time of the year when evil is greatest," Heihachi explained.

"The longest night," Kanbei scratched his head, considering the events of the morning. "Perhaps it is not strange to think that the *oni* would come out on this day."

"Do you think I was attacked because of the Solstice?" I asked Heihachi, finally forgetting the monkey momentarily and joining the conversation.

"The veil between this world and the next is the thinnest at these times," he replied, a wrinkle forming between his eyebrows. "It is possible."

"But what do we do now?" I asked.

"Blue *oni* gather together on certain days," Heihachi explained. "They share information on those days. The one that attacked you will tell the other *oni* in his clan about you." His tone was serious.

"What happens then?" Ken said, asking the question that was on my mind.

"Usually not much," he answered.

"We are afraid that the *oni* might have licked her," Kanbei said gravely. Immediately Heihachi's mood darkened.

"Ah. I see," Heihachi said. His demeanor changed as he considered the seriousness of the situation.

"Unfortunately," Heihachi began, "blue *oni* seem to have something of a blood lust. Once it has tasted your blood it becomes obsessed."

"Obsessed?" I asked.

"Yes, it won't stop until it has eaten you."

My mouth went dry. I didn't know what to say and even if I did I wasn't sure I could speak if I wanted to. My head was spinning.

"That's awful," I finally stammered.

"It gets worse. If it did in fact taste you it will pass on...your..." Heihachi paused to think of the correct word in English "... your DNA signature to the other blue *oni*."

'That can't be good,' I thought.

"Then the problem will only get worse," Katsushiro said, confirming my fears.

"The blue *oni* gather on *tai-an-bi*," Heihachi said.

"*Tai-an-bi*?" I asked.

"Certain days of the month," Heihachi replied.

"I thought *tai-an-bi* were supposed to be good days," Ken said. I was impressed. He had learned something in school. I looked at him. He shrugged.

"Depends on how you look at it," Heihachi said. "These days have long been known as auspicious days since the chance of meeting a blue *oni* is zero. All the *oni* are underground meeting with their clans. Good day for people."

"How often are *tai-an-bi*?" I asked.

"It is easier to see on a calendar," Heihachi said.

He turned and reached towards the desk. I thought he was going to pull out one of the scrolls that were scattered on his desk, but he just moved the scrolls and boxes out of the way. He pushed a button and a large computer monitor hummed to life. He touched the screen in a few places and quickly pulled up a calendar.

"The next *tai-an-bi* is here," he said pointing to the online calendar.

"That's the day after tomorrow!" I blurted out.

"That doesn't give us much time," Katsushiro said.

"Tomorrow at midnight the blue *oni* will gather with its clan and share the information about you."

"What happens then?" I asked.

"Then they come looking for you. Like ants to a picnic they will be coming after you." Heihachi's words hung in the air for a moment. Kanbei scowled at him. Catching the older samurai's look, Heihachi's expression changed and his eyes darted towards me. He shrugged.

"What can we do?" I asked.

"That's easy. Hit the road Jack," Heihachi replied. Despite the seriousness of the situation, I laughed at his choice of English phrases. "The safest thing is for you to leave Japan."

"Could I ever come back?" I asked.

"No. The *oni* will tell its clan and the information will spread from clan to clan. Each *tai-an-bi* will increase the danger. Eventually the taste of you will be passed from *oni* to *oni* until all *oni* throughout the country know. You won't be safe anywhere in

Japan," Heihachi said. His smile had vanished with the weight of what he was saying.

Kyuzo watched silently. I saw the grim look on his face in the dim light of the monitor.

"Normally the *oni* are not aggressive and will leave most people alone," Heihachi continued. "They are reluctant to expose themselves too much. Without the DNA problem you might have been able to stay in the country as long as you avoided shrines and the holy places."

"And the subway," Katsushiro added helpfully.

"Yes," Heihachi continued. "But because they have tasted your DNA they will not rest until they have finished you off. The *oni* become very aggressive in this case. Vindictive really. They will leave the usual places and act together as a group...even moving around in broad daylight. Little is known about this kind of behavior."

"*If* they have tasted..." Ken corrected.

"What?" Heihachi asked distractedly.

"*If* they have tasted her DNA. We don't know for sure that it licked her," Ken explained.

"Ah, yes, I see. Of course," Heihachi corrected himself. "*If* they have tasted your skin and acquired your DNA, then they will surely track you down."

"Wait a minute," I said desperately. "Can't you swab my arm? Test the wound? Look for some *oni* saliva? Can't you do something?"

"This is the theater, Maya. Not CSI," Heihachi replied. "We won't know for sure if the blue *oni* has come into contact with your blood."

"It is too dangerous for you," Kanbei said. "You can't risk it."

"Maya, you will never be able to come back to Japan," Katsushiro said. He sounded sad.

I felt light headed. The thought of leaving my life here – of leaving my dad – made my head swim. Telling my dad about the *oni* attack was bad enough. I couldn't imagine telling him that I had to leave the country on top of that. He would kill me. How was I even going to get him to believe me about the *oni* in the first place? I felt sick. I gritted my teeth together to keep from feeling nauseated.

"You said that was my *safest* option. What are the other options?" I asked.

"Pardon me?"

"If that was the safest option, there must be other options."

"Uh..." Heihachi thought for a moment. I waited with clenched teeth, trying not to be sick. "The other option would be to kill that *oni*. Or if we can't get to it by midnight tomorrow, to kill its clan."

"How many *oni* are in its clan?" Ken asked. Despite being younger than I was, he was being coldly practical in his thinking about the situation.

"Hard to say," Heihachi replied. "We don't know all that there is to know about blue *oni*. Most clans seem to be seven or eight *oni* strong."

"Seven or eight!" I sputtered. I couldn't imagine how bad that would be. "That one blue *oni* in the park almost killed us. It would have too, if Kanbei and Katsushiro hadn't saved us. Seven or eight?"

There was a moment of silence. I was trying to get my head around the gravity of the situation. I didn't know what to say.

"We should do it," Ken said. I was surprised at how determined he sounded. He had that look on his face that he got before he got into fights at school. His hands were clenched tightly into fists.

"Ken, we..." I started to protest.

"Would you guys help us?" Ken asked, ignoring me for the moment. I realized he was serious about this.

"Yes," Kanbei said. I couldn't believe he was taking Ken seriously. He had answered immediately, without hesitation.

"I would too," said Katsushiro earnestly.

Kyuzo had been quiet until then, but now he protested. "They are not ready to fight yet." He was talking about me and Ken. "It is too soon."

"They need our help," Katsushiro said, turning on Kyuzo. He was the one who got emotional quickly. I could see his face flush as he spoke. I liked that about him. He clenched his square jaw.

"We have to help them." His voice tried unsuccessfully for a persuasive note. I admired him for his passionate desire to help us.

"It's not a matter of us helping them," Kyuzo shot back. "They aren't ready."

"This means we will be outnumbered," Kanbei said quietly, scratching his head. He had done the math. The group turned to look at Heihachi.

"You know how I feel about *oni*," Heihachi said, shaking his head. His face turning quite pale.

"It wouldn't be right for us to ask you to..." I started out, but I was interrupted.

"What? This is the reason we became samurai," Katsushiro went on forcefully. "Didn't we all swear to fight evil? To protect people like Ken and Maya." His face glowed with his emotions. "We have to help them."

"I'm in," Heihachi said, straightening his shoulders. His idiomatic English surprised me again.

"It is too dangerous for *them*," Kyuzo threw out, unpersuaded.

Kanbei paused for a moment, weighing this. Then he said, "It should be their decision."

"You guys," I protested. "There is no way we can fight seven or eight *oni*. We'll all get killed."

"We don't have a choice," Ken said, ignoring the samurai and speaking to me. "As long as those things are out there they are going to be after you. Who knows how far they will go? We'll never know if you are safe. I would rather face them down now than have you live in fear for the rest of your life."

I had to admit he had a point. I didn't want this thing chasing me for the rest of my life. I began to understand his motives. I wondered if this is why Ken got in to so many fights at school. He would rather fight out the problem now than leave it to boil slowly. I thought of what it would be like to live my life wondering if an *oni* was around the corner or would pop up in the subway somewhere to terrorize me. I imagined my life played out in fear.

Ken looked strong, but I could see that there were almost tears in his eyes.

"Maya, I can't let anything happen to you. I won't."

I had never seen my brother speak with such determination. His eyes were shining, and I could see that he was focused on a singular purpose. I was that purpose. Keeping me safe.

Ken, Katsushiro and Kanbei were committed as well. Even Heihachi had thrown his lot in with us now too. The last to commit was the stoic Kyuzo. His face was stony, betraying no emotion. I looked into his eyes to see if I could catch any glimpse of how he was feeling. Unmoving, he stared back at me, while the group waited in silent expectation. We all knew we would need his skill if we were going to make this work.

"When do we leave?" Kyuzo said at last.

I breathed a sigh of relief, and a sense of anticipation spread through the group. I could feel the change in the room now that Kyuzo had said he would help us.

"Is there any way we could win?" I asked, voicing the question that was on everyone's minds.

Heihachi answered, "Maybe." I could see the gears turning in his mind as he tried to riddle out the best strategy for the fight.

"We would have to strike them swiftly," he said. "Once provoked, blue *oni* only get more vicious."

"What's the best way to kill an *oni*?" I asked.

"The way you don't die," Heihachi said flatly.

"An attack on an *oni* clan." Kanbei's voice was grave. "Not many have lived to talk about that."

"Not many. But some have done it," Heihachi said, but there was no optimism in his voice. "If any can succeed, it would be these two." I wasn't sure if Heihachi was just being complimentary or if there was something more. I wondered what he was talking about. I started to ask, but Ken interrupted.

"What if we got them to come to us?"

"An ambush?" Kanbei said. I could see he was weighing the idea. He scratched the stubble on his head as he thought, pacing the room as he considered the concept.

"Maybe if they didn't know you were on our side," Ken said. My brother was proving to be particularly good at strategy, and I could tell the samurai thought so too. When he made a suggestion, I could see they thought about it carefully.

"If they thought it was just me and Maya, it would catch them off guard," Ken suggested.

"We could hide and let them come in close," Kyuzo said, thinking the plan through. His hand was resting on the hilt of his sword, and I saw it tighten and relax as he spoke.

"The *oni* might overlook our presence," Katsushiro said slowly. "If they were hungry enough..."

"Or angry enough."

"Their confidence would work in our favor," Kanbei considered this plan.

"There are ways to distract them from our scent as well," Heihachi added.

Determined to find a way to save me, the samurai began talking to each other in Japanese very quickly. I could see their excitement building.

"It just might work," Kanbei said at last switching back to English for our benefit. "But we don't have much time."

We decided we would spend the night at the Palace and then go to our house in the morning. We would have a day to prepare and then expect the attack at night. Kanbei believed the timing was tight but it could be done.

"Maya," Kanbei said. "Your house is on the Koshu-kaido, which stretches to Kai-no-kuni."

"Koshu-kaido?" I asked.

"It is one of the five routes in and out of Edo," Katsushiro offered.

"Edo?"

"Er, Tokyo," he said correcting himself. "Hatsudai – where you live," he went on, "is along the Koshu-kaido. These are the old routes, preserved since ancient times. These routes have been used by both people and *oni*."

That the ancient routes were familiar to *oni* as well as humans came as something of a surprise to me. Katsushiro explained that these roadways were hundreds of years old. Over time, the paths had become roads. And the roads had become highways. The concrete highway that I knew followed the path of the ancient Koshu-kaido.

"Yes, this will work to our advantage," Kanbei said.

My heart was conflicted by the prospect of all of this. On one hand, I felt the cold hand of terror as I thought about the *oni* that had attacked me and the prospect of facing this terrible creature again. When I remembered the horrible smell and thought about being eaten alive, I shuddered. On the other hand, I was ready to get it over with. I hated the thought of living my life in fear. Win or lose I wanted to get to a resolution. Continuing on in limbo like this was not an option for me. And how would my family survive?

"Ken, you had better call Dad," I said after our plans were settled.

He pulled his phone out of his pocket and dialed Dad's number. Even though it was late, Dad was still at the office. It didn't surprise me at all. He was obsessed with his work, and it seemed to me he was hiding from our family life. I was sure he hadn't even noticed we were gone.

"Dad," Ken started and then went on breathlessly not waiting for him to respond. "Maya got attacked by an *oni* so we are hanging out with some samurai. We are going to stay at the Emperor's Palace and then get home tomorrow."

I couldn't hear what Dad was saying on the other end of the line. Ken nodded a few times.

"Okay," Ken said and then hung up.

"I think he took it well," Ken said to me.

"What did he say?" I asked incredulously. I couldn't believe Dad had reacted so calmly.

"He said to be sure we got our homework done before we did any more video games."

"What?" I asked. I couldn't believe it. Well, maybe I could. I'm sure my father was only half listening to Ken and for the small portion that he did hear, he interpreted as talk about some video game.

"Oh, do you guys have any video games at your house?" Heihachi asked hopefully.

With that, we left Kabuki-za and walked out into the cold air on our way back to the Palace. We were quiet. I stumbled along exhausted from the long and tiring day.

"*Sugei hara heta*," Heihachi said to me as we walked.

"Huh?" I asked him not understanding.

"I'm starving!" he repeated in English rubbing his stomach for emphasis.

"Yeah, me too," Ken piped up. We had not eaten since our snack in the Palace.

"Do you like sushi?" Kanbei asked us.

"Yes!" Ken and I replied in unison without hesitation. We loved sushi. I explained that it was one of our favorites and that our father took us often since we had moved to Tokyo. With that it was decided we would stop at a sushi shop that Kanbei knew.

Kanbei lead us to restaurant which was dimly lit and smelled like the ocean. A handful of customers dotted the tables and chairs, while one man worked behind the counter. By this point my thinking had changed so dramatically that I wasn't concerned about walking into the restaurant with our samurai armor and swords at our sides. We found space at the sushi bar, which was empty except for a woman in a *kimono*, who sat with her back to us at the far end of the counter. I chose the seat closest to the door next to Kanbei. Ken was several seats away from me still talking to Heihachi about video games.

The man behind the counter wore a blue *jinbei* and a purple and white *hachimaki* twisted into a headband. He had short black hair and a keen eye, watching everything in the shop carefully. Who was finished? Who still looked hungry? He stood guard over a glass case that contained some of the freshest looking fish I'd seen. There were several kinds of fish. Some I knew. Many I didn't recognize. I saw shrimp and all kinds of shell fish. Crabs and clams. I was so hungry that everything looked good.

Grabbing a small bit of warm rice in his hands, the sushi chef quickly formed it into a small ball. He wrapped the fish around the rice and squeezed quickly, binding the rice together and creating an ideal bite-sized morsel. My mouth watered at the sight.

Behind him an impressive array of lacquer bowls and ceramic plates were stacked on a shelf. Long skinny plates for sashimi. Small round plates for soy sauce. His hand hovered over all the plates before selecting one that was right for the occasion. He brought it down and artfully arranged his sushi creations on it.

Finishing with that task, he picked up a knife with a wooden handle. The light of the room caught the blade and flashed briefly in my direction.

"Looks razor sharp," I said absently mindedly.

Kanbei nodded but said nothing.

I watched the chef take out a piece of fish from the case. From where I sat it looked as if he merely set the knife on the edge of the block of fish. The blade was so sharp it sliced through the flesh without any effort from the chef, as if the weight of the knife alone was enough to make the cut.

Catching me staring, the sushi chef motioned at the sword stuck in Kanbei's belt and said something in Japanese which I didn't understand. Kanbei threw back his head and laughed. The other samurai laughed too. (Except for the stoic Kyuzo who only smiled.) The samurai chatted amiably with the sushi chef who nodded and laughed good-naturedly as he quickly and skillfully assembled one bite-sized creation after another for us.

Reaching over the top of the counter, he deposited the sushi pieces in front of each of us on a black lacquer plate. His hands were a blur as he crafted bite-size sushi morsels for each of us in rapid succession.

I worked my way through all of my favorites: tuna, shad, salmon, and mackerel before moving on to new delights like scallop and clam. The highlight of the meal was a fresh eel which the chef had prepared with sake and soy sauce. The result was a sparkling jewel on my plate that dissolved in my mouth, a moment of pure sushi happiness momentarily allowing me to forget my troubles.

With the renewed perspective on life that comes with a full stomach, I looked around the sushi restaurant with fresh eyes while the samurai continued to eat. In the dim light, I turned my attention to the woman in the *kimono* sitting at the opposite end of the counter. With her back still towards me, I had a generous view of the elaborate brocade work on the *obi* around her waist. On it, lazy orange carp swam downstream under blue and green lilies which floated in its rich silk pattern. The woman's long, black hair was neatly coiffed with a variety of lacquered pins and ornaments. I couldn't imagine wrestling my own brown hair into such perfect order. With her left hand she absentmindedly twirled one of the pins in her hair, and with her right hand she held a long slender pipe, which she was smoking distractedly. The pipe was made of bamboo but had a worn metal mouth piece at one end and a small metal bowl at the other. Rings of smoke drifted upward slowly, only to disappear eventually into the dark air above her head.

As if sensing me staring at her – in that peculiar way that people do when you stare at their back for long enough – she looked about and then turned in my direction. When she did, my heart froze. Instead of the face of a woman, she had the head of a fish – a carp. Her neck was human – and her long black hair too – but her face was that of a fish. I gasped outwardly and studied the rest of her. She was all woman. And by that, I mean that her body, her arms, her legs all appeared to be human. It was only her face that was fish. It might have been all of her head but much of it was covered by her thick black hair. The orange scaly face protruded out from under the carefully groomed hair and she scowled at me with brown fish eyes, still twirling the pin in her hair with her human hand.

I held my breath. Was she a threat? Just as I was wondering this, she yawned and stuck the long slender pipe back into her fish mouth. Even in the dimly lit sushi bar, I could make out her cartilaginous fish teeth. She puffed on the pipe twice before the smoke escaped from her gills – where her ears would have been. Slowly turning her fish head away from me, she studied the other customers in the restaurant.

"Um..." I started to interrupt the samurai who were still conversing amiably with the sushi chef.

"Does anyone see that woman?" I asked. Kanbei and the other samurai turned to look.

"Which woman?" Kanbei asked.

"The customer there at the end of the counter," I hissed.

"Oh?" He studied her for a moment. "That's not a customer."

"I know, right?" I felt vindicated. "It's some kind of fish creature—"

"No, she works here," Kanbei interrupted me. Without giving it a second thought, he returned to talking to the chef behind the counter.

Because Kanbei's nonchalance told me I had nothing to fear, I continued to eat, but I could not take my eyes off of the odd fish-woman working at the sushi bar.

The sushi was delicious, even to my inexperienced palate, and we had eaten hungrily. In the chef's hands each perfectly plump grain of rice exploded with flavor. Each expertly sliced strip of fish married to the rice at the hand of the sushi chef. The chef, having singlehandedly completed the task of feeding all of us, was eager to talk to me.

"Balance is everything in the creation of sushi," he told me, as he paused in front of me, leaning over the counter to see how I had enjoyed his meal. "Too much rice and you cannot eat it. It won't fit in your mouth." He laughed a little at foolishness of this mistake, before continuing, "Too little and it is overpowered by the fish."

"But the real art," he said and here his voice fell to a conspiratorial whisper causing me to lean forward, "Is how you cut the fish." His eyes darted to the side. I followed his gaze to the fish woman in the *kimono* at the other end of the counter.

"What are you saying?" the fish woman suddenly yelled, shaking a fist and knocking down the tea by her elbow. The tranquil nature of the sushi bar evaporated.

"I don't like it when you tell secrets," she huffed. She suspected he was talking about her and became visibly upset, her gills flaring angrily.

I shook my head. "No, no. We weren't telling secrets," I was about to say, but before I could get this out the fish woman started shouting at the sushi chef again.

"Have you been lying to those customers?" she demanded.

"I have not," he declared hotly. Now he was as mad as she was. I watched it all with wide eyes.

"No one wants to hear your stupid fish tales," she yelled at the man, her voice quickly reaching an angry pitch.

"I wasn't telling fish tales," the man shot back angrily. He was as accustomed to her angry tone as he was to everything else in the shop.

I saw him reach across the counter and pick up his razor-sharp knife as he continued to glare angrily at the fish-woman. I wasn't sure how he intended to use it. Instantly, Kanbei was standing at my side. He gently grabbed my arm and pulled me up from my seat at the bar.

"Perhaps this is our signal to leave," he said quietly in my ear, maneuvering me towards the exit.

"I think you might be right," I stuttered, dumbfound at the strange turn of events at the sushi restaurant. The altercation continued as our party left the restaurant.

There is a Japanese saying I have since learned which says, "The best relationships are thick with arguments." I've come to believe that to be true.

Outside the air was cold on my skin. Kanbei led us through the streets back towards the Palace. It was late evening now and the streets were full. Good-natured people were finishing work or were saying goodbye after a night out with their friends. For these people life went on much as it always had.

Katsushiro came up beside me as we walked. He said nothing. I said nothing. We just walked in silence. Somehow it felt safer having him beside me.

Walking briskly, we arrived at the Palace and entered through the Seimon Gate. The guard there recognized our party and bowed deeply. I wondered about the hierarchy of the samurai. Kanbei had spoken with such deference about the *hatamoto*. And this guard seemed to know our samurai and treated them with respect. What was it like to live in a hierarchical society like this?

I would have given it more thought, but after the events of the day, Ken and I were exhausted. The samurai gave us warm clothes for sleeping and provided us with *futon* bedding in a small quiet room. I had been anxious when I crawled under the covers, but I was so exhausted by our adventures that I was sure I would fall asleep quickly. The mental strain of the day – fearing for my life – and the physical exertion of the walk had left me spent.

Ken was in the *futon* bed next to mine. I could just make out his features in the dimly lit room.

"Maya?" he called out my name. Squinting, I saw a peculiar look on his face. Or was it the light? "Remember the dreams I used to have?"

"What are you talking about, Ken?"

"Before. Don't you remember? Those terrible dreams I used to have when I was a kid."

"Everybody has scary dreams," I replied, distracted by my own thoughts. I vaguely remembered Ken having bad dreams when we lived in America. He had become afraid of the dark after we moved away from Japan the first time.

"Not like this." His face was deadly serious as he went on. His tone gave me pause. "Do you remember that little dresser that was in our room?"

"What dresser?" I asked, propping myself up on one elbow to see him better.

"The one with the drawers. The one that..." his voice trailed off. I knew what he was going to say. He was going to say, "The one that Mom gave us" but he didn't.

"Yeah sure. I remember it. It was in our room." I didn't want to talk about Mom right now either, but I remembered the antique dresser. It was a hand-made wooden piece with black metal fittings on the corners and black metal handles as well. The ancient wooden drawers each had a metal lock but the key had long been lost. The drawers were locked but for some reason my father had kept it in the house anyways.

"I used to have a dream about a little man who came out of that dresser during the night. He was an old man," Ken said in an eerie far-away voice.

"Old – but he didn't seem old," Ken went on. "He had a long nose over a dirty beard and ugly yellow fingernails. And, this was the strangest thing, he had feathers on his back."

"What? Like an angel?"

"No, not like that. Black feathers. Dirty and dark. And not quite wings. The worst part about it was his yellow eyes. He had shining yellow eyes. Angry eyes."

"So, you had scary dreams when you were a kid," I said. "So what. No big deal. I did too."

"This was different, Maya." Ken said it quietly, almost as if he was back in the dream now. "Every night he would come out of the dresser. He came to see me. He came to see me, Maya. I would hide under the covers but he would wait for me. I could hear him clucking his teeth. It was a terrible noise, almost as if he had a beak. Clack. Clack. Clack. I was terrified. If I looked out he would be there, staring at me, cocking his head from side to side. Every night he would return." Ken ended. His voice drifted away.

"Why didn't you ever say anything about this?" I asked. "Why didn't you ever tell me?"

"Somehow I knew," Ken explained, "I don't know how I knew this but I knew that if I told you about it, he would come to see you too."

"That makes my spine tingle, Ken." I told him.

"The dreams eventually stopped," Ken said. "They ended when we moved. Somehow the dresser never came with us."

Nodding, I tried to think what had happened to that dresser. I clearly remembered it, but I couldn't recall where I had seen it last. In any event, I hadn't seen it for years.

Ken was lost in thought, caught between a dream and reality. It was as if he had one foot in both worlds. Still fully awake, I looked at his face carefully as he drifted off. He stared quietly into the distance, as if he could still see it. The room was eerily quiet. So much so that it surprised me when he started talking again.

"Here's the strangest part," he told me. "After that move, the dreams stopped. I never saw him after that. Until last night. Last night I saw him again. He came to see me."

"Ken, I..." I didn't know what to say. I couldn't shake the feeling that I had let him down. I stared at the ceiling in the darkness for a while, and when I turned back to Ken he was asleep. I watched him breathing softly until drowsiness finally descended on me, and then, unable to stay awake another moment longer, I fell asleep.

I awoke with a start. In the *futon* across from me, Ken lay in deep sleep.

"Ken?" I whispered. No response. I wondered if he was dreaming about the yellow-eyed man. I saw the covers rise and fall with the rhythm of his breathing. He was too peaceful to be having a nightmare.

Silently I pushed back the *futon* that covered me and tiptoed to the *shoji* door. I slid it open quietly. A pair of house slippers were in the hall waiting for me. I slipped them on, exiting on padded feet. The hall was cold compared to the warmth of my bed but not as cold as it had been during the day. I shivered once then followed the long corridor, closing the *shoji* door behind me. The wooden floor creaked slightly under my feet. Turning the corner, I found myself in unexplored territory within the Palace. I had no destination in mind – just wandering in the dark hallways.

Creeping through the eerie blackness of the unknown place, I couldn't help thinking I was trespassing on its sacred grounds. I worried about the punishment for wandering the Palace without an escort. I knew that my samurai – and by now I felt close enough to Kanbei and the others to think of us as being part of the same team – would scold me for wandering without an escort but knew that they would not be truly cross with me. However, I didn't know about the other samurai in the Palace. I wondered what would happen to me if I were caught.

At the end of a long hallway I found a golden *fusuma* door and paused in front of it for a moment wondering if it protected untold treasure. Perhaps the Emperor himself was sleeping nearby. If so, I couldn't help wondering if his sleep was as fitful as mine. Were his thoughts troubled by some crises of state? Or by dreams of *oni*? Feeling more daring than a trespasser in the Imperial Palace should, I opened the golden *fusuma* door wondering if I was throwing light on some sacred relic of the world's oldest uninterrupted empire.

I was surprised to see a woman sitting alone in the room. She wore a white *kimono* that almost seemed to glow. It had a pattern woven into the fabric. This too was white. White on white. Kneeling in front of a small table, she tended a fire that had been kindled inside a *ro* – a sort of small fireplace contrived in the floor of the room. Quietly tending to her work, she moved slowly – patiently – trying to coax a flame from the reluctant coals.

"Oh, I'm sorry. I didn't think anyone was awake," I said nonchalantly, but inwardly panicked to be caught snooping.

"Take off your shoes, Maya."

"Pardon me?"

"Take off your shoes. This room is special. You must leave your shoes outside," she said. Her voice was small, barely more than a whisper, but she spoke with such authority that I couldn't help doing as I was told. Obediently, I left the slippers outside and entered barefoot. With her free hand she made a gracious gesture, unmistakably suggesting I sit. I knelt down quietly on the fresh *tatami* mat. The embers of the fire struggled faintly between us.

"I'm afraid I'm rather lost," I said, trying to cover the fact that I had been wandering unescorted in the Palace.

She paused from her task for a moment and looked up from the fire to observe me. She stared at me briefly while I squirmed.

"This room is not easily discovered," she said after a time, returning her gaze to the would-be fire. She looked young, perhaps a little older than me. Her jet-black hair was tied up. Her hand patiently worked the coals. "You would not have found it unless it was meant to be."

I wondered if she meant that in the "universe brought us together" sort of way. Or maybe there was something more to it than that?

"I guess I couldn't sleep," I said, wondering if I should bring up the events of the day. Would she believe me if I did?

"You've been dreaming about the *oni*," she said. She knew about our experiences in the shrine. The samurai must have told her.

"I have," I confessed. "I'm very afraid of those terrible blue monsters." Thoughts of fangs and talons exploded into my mind like a firecracker as they had done all day. I closed my eyes, willing my brain to think of something else. Daisies. Dandelions. Puppies. It was no use. A blue fear gripped my heart, and I shuddered. I knew it was me they were hunting.

"The danger is neither more nor less than it was the day before," she said in her whisper-voice, not looking up from the fire which now looked to be on the verge of going out. "It's just that you understand it better now."

"But the monster – the *oni*—it's out to get me," I protested.

"The monster was there yesterday. The difference is that you see it now. Before you were unaware, but now your eyes have been opened."

I thought for a moment about her words and decided to change the subject.

"They say that the Emperor of Japan is descended from the gods."

"All leaders derive their power from divine mandate," she replied confidently in her firm voice. If she was annoyed that I had changed the subject, she didn't let on. She flipped a grey coal over to expose its orange glowing face.

"Does the Emperor know about the *oni*?" I asked.

"Of course," she said, looking up at me with surprise. Then her expression changed as an angry look flickered across her face. "They have contaminated this land." I was taken aback by the sudden venom in her words.

"Why doesn't the Emperor do something?" I couldn't help but notice the tone of accusation in my own voice.

She looked at me in surprise again. "But he *has* done something," she replied as if she was explaining something obvious. "He has charged the samurai with protecting the people. He has a plan, Maya." She paused. Then noticing the puzzled look on my face, added for clarification, "*We* are the plan."

I thought about this for a moment. The samurai had indeed saved us. And they were working to help us now. Was this the Emperor's plan to protect his people? She had said, "*We* are the plan." What did that mean? I wondered if I was part of that plan. How could I be? What could one girl do against those terrible monsters? I continued to think but didn't know what to say.

"What is this?" I asked, pointing to a small object behind her. It looked to be a mirror but it was no modern mirror. It was made of metal and was elaborately worked. The surface had been polished so that it clearly reflected the room. I marveled at the Japanese command of ancient technology. It was a superb artifact and looked like it belonged in a museum.

"There are three sacred objects of our empire," the woman said, not looking up from the fire. "This is one of them."

"It's so beautiful."

"It is a mirror," she said softly, still absorbed in her task. "It reflects the world as it truly is. It is a symbol of the wisdom the Emperor requires to rule his people. He must see things as they really are."

Considering her words, I paused. Neither of us said anything for a while. We just sat quietly in the room listening to the crackling noise of the coals. Finally breaking the silence, I said, "I guess I've been pretty blind to all the terrible things in the world."

"Yes, and now your eyes have been opened," she said exposing another orange-faced coal.

"I don't wish my fate on anyone," I let out under my breath. Thinking of the *oni* that I had encountered that day, I was beginning to feel sorry for myself.

"Nothing in this world happens by chance, Maya. Now it is your fate to serve the Emperor. You must rid our land of this terrible *oni*. The lot has fallen on you."

"I'm just one girl. What can I do?" I was ready to give up.

"Look in the mirror, Maya," she said gesturing to the object behind her with the tongs she held in her hand. "What do you see? A scared little girl? Or a woman ready for battle? Do you see a fugitive? Or a warrior? Someone who is ready to run? Or someone ready to rid this land of the *oni*?"

I looked in the mirror and wondered if I was up to the challenge. It was just my face. I looked the way I always looked. Brown bangs. Freckles. A bit tired, perhaps.

"I'm not sure," I told her as truthfully as I could. Somehow, I knew there was no point in being anything but utterly honest with this woman.

"Maya, your role in all of this is yet to be seen." Her words hung in the quiet of the small room.

The coals in the little fire glowed brightly now. The woman sat back, apparently pleased with her work. Her task accomplished, she smiled and looked up at me. I felt a warm golden glow in my veins.

"Maya, the morning is still some ways off. You should go back to sleep." The minute she said it, drowsiness descended on me, and I remembered how tired I was. I tried to stifle the yawn I felt, but it slipped out anyway.

"Yes, maybe you're right," I mumbled, but it was all I could do to keep my eyes open. Feeling half asleep, I bowed to the woman, found my slippers where I had left them by the door and stumbled back to my room.

Returning through the halls in a fog, I collapsed onto the *futon*, turning the words of the woman in the white *kimono* over in my head. The Emperor had a plan, she had said. "And *we* are the plan." I couldn't help wondering if it was right to include me in that 'we'.

Ken was right where I had left him, asleep in the *futon* next to mine, still breathing quietly. A small part of me wanted to wake him to talk about the woman in the white *kimono*, but I knew he needed sleep as badly as I did. Without an excuse to stay awake, sleep closed in quickly.

113

Exhausted by the events of the day, I pulled the warm cover of my *futon* up over me and fell asleep as soon as my head hit the pillow. It felt like the deepest sleep, but I remember having the most vivid dream. Even now, years later, I still recall that dream in great detail.

To be honest, as I think back, it's almost difficult to distinguish between the dream and the other events of my life at that time. Everything was so surreal. It's as if the dream were as real as the rest of the things that were happening to me then.

In my dream, I woke up to a strange noise. It was a flute, a bamboo flute. Soon the flute was joined by a muffled chant, sounding like some kind of dirge. The sliding *fusuma* doors by the foot of my bed were parted slightly, and the noise was clearly coming from the room next door. A dim light flickered through the door.

Throwing off my covers, I got up to investigate and tiptoed over to the door to take a peek. Quietly, I inched closer and looked through the gap in the doors to the next room.

I saw the source of the light. Several candles on stands gave a flickering glow to the room. In the shadows, men moved about. They wore the white smocks and black hats that I would learn later were the characteristic garb of Shinto clergy. There were twelve of them in the room performing some sort of ritual, moving around like mourners. The chant was coming from them.

One priest adjusted the candles. Another tended to a censer from which a warm sweet-smelling smoke drifted. It was too dark to make out the faces of the priests. I wondered if the samurai we knew were there, but their identities were hidden in the shadows.

I could tell – as one knows things in a dream – that the priests were performing this ritual for someone in the corner. I could see that someone was there, but that person was just out of my view to the right. Was it the Emperor?

I tried to lean to the left so that I could get a peek at whoever was sitting there, but a small screen on the floor obscured by view. No matter how hard I tried to get a glimpse, I couldn't see.

Just at that moment, leaning forward, I put my hand on the *fusuma* door which separated our room and hid me. As I did, the door made a slight rattling sound. Immediately the priests stopped and stared at me. All eyes were on me.

114

"Oh no," I said in a whisper. "I don't belong here." In my dream, I was overcome with a feeling of being out of place. I was an intruder in a world that I didn't understand. This was a place for samurai, not for a kid like me. I was an interloper in a feudal system that had gone on for 1000 years. My hands started to shake.

Two of the priests pulled open a sliding door on the far side of the room. Beyond the doors lay another room and in this room I saw many samurai kneeling quietly.

"I don't think I can do this," I said to myself. One of the priests standing closest to me stepped closer. I turned and looked for a way out, but I couldn't find it. I wanted to get away, but I had the horrible feeling of being unable to run.

Immediately, Kanbei, who was kneeling in the other room, emerged from the ranks of the kneeling samurai and walked over to me. He moved confidently, and his presence encouraged me.

"In service to the Emperor," I whispered.

When I looked up at his face, I could see that he was speaking, but no words came out. I could not hear what he was saying. It was if someone had turned the volume down on the TV. I tried to focus, hoping to understand what he was trying to tell me. I looked at his lips.

"Wa-"something. "Ma-" something. What was he saying? Then I got it. "Wake up, Maya."

"What?"

"Wake up, Maya." It was Kanbei, poking his head into the room where Ken and I were sleeping. "It's time to get up," he said.

Yawning through a groggy fog, I sat up in my *futon* and blinked my surprise at the transition between dream and wakefulness. Beside me, Ken shook the sleep from his head and sat up in his *futon* in the dim dawn light. I moved slowly at first, but then when our plan for the day came to mind, I snapped fully awake. With that, Ken and I got up from our beds and launched into preparations for the day.

## Chapter Six
## A Quiet Evening at Home

By the time Ken and I folded our *futon* bedding, the samurai were already busy in preparation in the next room. I noted the determination on their faces as they made themselves ready. It wasn't grim but it was – what should I call it? Resigned to the genuine possibility that today might very well be their last day of life. It was, I was to learn later, a common predicament for the samurai.

"We should get there as quickly as possible," Kanbei told us. "Katsushiro, will you prepare the bikes?" He said it with the authority and confidence to which I had become accustomed.

"*Ha!*" the young samurai said with a bow and quickly walked out of the room.

"Heihachi?" Kanbei continued.

"Yes, sir?" the young samurai replied, stepping forward with a slight bow to Kanbei.

"Find us a map of the area around Ken and Maya's home."

"Yes, sir!" and Heihachi disappeared from the room.

"Ken, Maya?"

"Yes, sir?" we said in unison. Kanbei's ability to lead compelled us.

"You need to dress. The armory will have anything else that you need." He paused expecting an answer from us and then, as if remembering, he pointed with a commanding gesture and continued, "The armory is down this hall on the left."

"Yes, sir!" we answered and immediately left to change. Behind us, Kanbei and Kyuzo began to talk urgently in Japanese. Their voices echoed in the hallway as we walked away, our stocking feet quiet on the polished wooden floors.

Looking at my reflection in the dark cherry-colored wood, a serious face stared back at me, my brown bangs hanging in my eyes.

"This is it," I said to the girl staring up at me.

When I entered the Palace's armory, I had expected a room like the supply store in Omote-Sando, but instead I found a quiet *tatami* room occupied only by an old man in a grey *kimono* who knelt in the middle of the floor, reverently addressing the wall to our right. He did not look at us when we opened the sliding door and walked in, but instead bowed his head to the ground in the direction of the wall. He looked ancient. He was easily the oldest person we had seen since we arrived at the Palace yesterday. He spoke to us in Japanese.

Ken and I looked at each other. The old man's tone was friendly enough, but neither of us understood a word he was saying. He paused, apparently waiting for an answer.

"We are here for *armor*," Ken tried in English.

The man quizzed us again in a volley of Japanese questions that neither of us understood. He turned his head our way but kept his eyes more or less fixed on the sliding screen in front of him.

"It's for a *battle*," Ken tried again, prompting another stream of Japanese from the man.

"It's against *oni*," I finally said.

"*Oni*?" the man said, this time turning towards us.

"Yes. *Hai. Oni*," I replied.

The old man bowed his head again and nodded before standing.

"*Oni ka*?" he said as if to himself.

I watched him as he moved from sitting to standing. He was strong and his body moved quickly, despite his age. It was at this moment that I happened to glance at his wrists which protruded from the sleeves of his *kimono*. They were thick and muscular. His hands seemed to me like they would be accustomed to wielding a sword, and I imagined them to be those of a retired warrior.

After he stood, he gestured at the floor where Ken and I were standing and said something in Japanese. Ken shot me a quizzical glance which I returned with a non-committal shrug. Without waiting for us to respond, the old man opened the sliding door of the wall, bowed one more time and disappeared, closing the doors behind him. We were left alone in the room.

"I think we are supposed to sit down," Ken said, mimicking my shrug.

We settled ourselves cross-legged on the floor and waited for the man to return. I looked at the sliding doors that he had been studying when we arrived. The doors themselves were unremarkable. While many of the doors and partitions in the Palace had sumptuous paintings, sporting images of trees, tigers, flowers, birds and mountains painted in mineral ink, these doors had no decoration at all. They were a solid color, with gold leaf applied to the entire surface. They were elegant but simple.

After a moment, the old man returned. He was flanked on either side by two young boys with twinkling eyes. The boys were half Ken's age and wore identical blue *kimono*. Their heads had been shaved. Despite their diminutive size, each carried a large wooden box which was easily more than half the size of its bearer.

Setting the boxes on the *tatami* mats in front of us, the boys took up positions behind each box. At this distance I could easily make out the grain of the wood which ran horizontally across the box. Black metal had been riveted to each corner to strengthen and protect. The boxes were well worn but clearly in good condition. Each lid was slightly larger than the base it rested on and reminded me of a certain large trunk I had once seen in my grandmother's house. The boys knelt behind the boxes – mirror images of boy and box, one for Ken and one for me. Each box came up to the shoulder of its kneeling boy.

Behind the boys, the old man shut the door and resumed his position on the *tatami* floor in the room, again staring at the blank golden sliding doors to our right so that we saw him in profile. He said a few words in Japanese, causing the boys to bow their shaved heads to the *tatami* mats before lifting the lids off of the boxes they had carried.

I peered into the wooden container set in front of me with great interest. Inside was a beautiful set of *o-yoroi*, armor. It was similar to the one that I had been wearing since shopping in Omote-Sando, but this one was ornate with carefully detailed handiwork. The surface looked like black lacquer and was polished to a reflective shine. I saw my reflection in the armor.

Well, I could see my nose and cheeks anyway. My eyes were dark pits in the shiny black lacquered surface.

"*Ii desu ka*?" I asked, pointing to the armor. *Is it okay?* I was grateful my rudimentary Japanese was coming in handy. I wasn't sure if should touch the armor, let alone use it. It looked so beautiful that I felt the need to ask.

The young boy in front of me turned to the old man and whispered to him in Japanese. The old man nodded without looking our way. Giving me a crooked smile, the boy waited for me to reach into the box in order to lift the armor before helping me with the task.

I put on a belt that included jet black panels that hung down and protected my waist and legs. Like an apron, it wrapped around my waist and was tied at the front. The boy taught me that the cuirass, the chest piece, was a *do*. When he held it up, I thought it too small for me, but when I got it on it was perfect – as if it had been meant for me. Hinged on the left, the *do* was supported by silk straps that went over my shoulders, like shoulder pads. Unlike the armor that I had acquired in Omote-Sando which was made up of several pieces braided together with silk cords, this was a single piece of well-shaped metal. This close I could see that the surface was not completely smooth but was decorated with an intricate design on the surface.

"It fits like a glove," I said laughing.

The boy smiled back at me. I wasn't sure if he understood my English.

"It really does fit perfectly," I thought, admiring the custom fit on my frame.

I looked over at Ken. He was almost ready as well, with a smaller black *do* covering his chest snugly. The individualized craftsmanship of the armor we wore was apparent, and I noted the variations in detail between Ken's suit and my own.

Finally, the boy helping me reached up to fasten on the shoulder guards of my armor. His young fingers moved quickly to tie the cords in order to secure it.

"Why is he staring at the screen?" I whispered to the boy who was helping me, nodding at the old man who was kneeling in the position he had been in when we entered the room.

"He does not stare at the screen," the boy said quietly, shaking his head gently. I picked up the slightest trace of an accent when he spoke.

"What is he staring at?" I asked.

"The garden."

"The garden?"

"You see the screen, but he sees the garden," the boy whispered back.

The boy looked at me and must have known that I didn't understand what he was talking about.

"The garden of the Emperor," the boy said smiling. He clearly assumed this was the explanation I needed. Guessing that there was a garden on the other side of the screen, I made a mental note to peek at it before we left.

When we were completely outfitted, we prepared to go. Before we left, the little boy who had been helping me leaned to the old man and informed him with a whisper that we were leaving. It was only then that I realized the old man was blind.

Years later – long after the old man's death – I finally returned to the Palace and by some chance found myself in that same room adjacent to the armory. Having long lost the reserve I'd felt in those early days, I pulled the golden doors open, convinced I'd find some beautiful garden worthy of the Emperor. Instead, I found the elegant doors opened only to an empty hallway, dark and utterly unremarkable.

When I meditate on the moment now, I often wish I had asked the blind old man to describe to me the Emperor's garden. I imagine it to be beautiful, and I would have loved to hear his description of it.

I have heard it said on more than one occasion that the line which separates this world from the next blurs shortly before one's death. I am convinced that the blind old man was looking into the next world in those last moments of his life, and I often wonder about the beauty of the garden which had so captured his attention.

At the time, however, my focus was only on the imminent threat from the awful blue *oni* and I was glad for the security of the protective armor which the old man gave us.

"*Arigato gozaimasu*," thank you, we said as we left. The old man, his eyes fixed on the unseen garden, remained seated but bowed deeply before we left.

Thinking back, I realize this was the second time that Ken and I had dressed in armor in as many days. Already it was becoming normal for me.

By the time we returned clad in our new *yoroi* armor, Kanbei had finished the preparations for our departure. The room was full of activity but surprisingly quiet. The samurai worked with near noiseless efficiency. I felt the seriousness of the path upon which we were about to embark.

Kanbei, Katsushiro, Heihachi and Kyuzo had all changed into battle gear as well. Their thick plated armor looked like variations of the getups that we were in. However, each black shiny chest piece of their armor had a golden crest in the middle, whereas ours was simply black without the crest. This was, I was to learn later, the Emperor's crest reserved for use by the Imperial Guard.

"Are we really going to bicycle back to our house?" Ken asked Kanbei as we walked into the Palace courtyard. I could sense his dread at the thought of a long bike-ride back, and I laughed to myself quietly. My brother the wimp, I thought.

"Not bicycle," Kanbei answered, handing me a black helmet. "Motorcycle."

Four jet black motorcycles were parked in a neat row in front of our building at the Palace. Although it was still early, the sun was shining brightly. The motorcycles, however, reflected almost no light. No chrome. No flashy paint. The four machines looked like nothing more than an inky black hole on fat black wheels. In full sunlight I could vaguely make out an engine and some sort of block-and-tube system that supported the wheels. In the shade these bikes would disappear.

"Ken, you are to ride with Katsushiro. Maya you are with Heihachi," Kanbei ordered.

"Hey guys, hang on." It was Ken, who wanted to get a photo of us with his phone before we left. Kanbei, Katsushiro, Heihachi and Kyuzo turned to face Ken. I was in the middle. The bikes were parked in the background.

"Got it," he said.

Years later when I examined this photo I was struck by how serene the samurai seemed, surrounding me there in front of their black motorcycles. Confident and radiant with a contentment I could not explain, they were almost smiling. I have contrasted that with my own worried expression in the photo. My frown betrays the stress of the moment for me – my skin drawn unusually tight – and my worries of *oni* written across my face.

I settled the black helmet on my head and got on the motorcycle behind Heihachi, swinging my leg up over the back of the bike and pulling myself into position behind him.

"Do you like Van Halen?" Heihachi asked me over his shoulder as I settled in. "I like Van Halen," he said before I could answer.

I fastened the chinstrap on my helmet.

The motorcycle roared to life and I dropped the helmet's visor down over my eyes. We rocketed out of the Palace behind Kanbei and Kyuzo.

Our helmets were outfitted with headphones and microphones. Eddie Van Halen's electric guitar erupted into my ears. Suddenly the sound was interrupted by Kanbei's voice.

"Maya, Ken, are you comfortable?"

"I am," Ken's voice came through a speaker in my helmet. I could see him clinging to Katsushiro on the back of his bike.

"Me too, sir."

"Good," was Kanbei's response. "Hang on. Gentlemen, let's stay tight. We don't need any excitement along the way."

All four bikes dropped into formation and accelerated past the Palace's inner moat. Leaning into each turn, the bikes hugged the road. I held on to Heihachi's waist. I could feel the samurai armor he was wearing. My chin hovered above his shoulder. On his armor in very small lettering was a blue smiley face with two horns and the phrase "have a nice day". I counted three hash marks under the smiley face.

"What is this?" I yelled hoping to be heard over the roar of the bikes. His voice came back loud in my ear. I had forgotten about the radio.

"*Oni* count," he explained. "Three and counting."

Speechless, I looked at the mark.

"You have run into three *oni* in Tokyo?" I asked.

"Not 'in' Tokyo. More like 'under' Tokyo," he said. "An *oni* caught me off-guard and knocked me out."

"Oh no, what did you do?" The thought of merely being close to an *oni* bothered me. The thought of being close to one while unconscious made positively nauseated me.

"When I woke up I was in its lair. It had dragged me underground."

He paused, obviously thinking about the experience. I didn't know how to respond.

"The monster was preparing a special celebration and I was going to be the guest of honor...or the main course," he laughed. "In any event I didn't stick around to find out. I chopped up as many of the blue buggers as I could and got the heck out of there."

"Is that why you know so much about *oni*?"

"Yup. I guess you could say it's a sick fascination with a dinner party from my past. One where I was on the menu." He had a genuine laugh and his words were casual – almost callous – but I could sense that he had been shaken by the experience.

"Okay, cut the chatter," came Kanbei's voice in my helmet. I had forgotten we were all on the same channel. His voice was stern on the speaker. "We are coming up on our exit."

The bikes zipped off the main road and rocketed down a narrow street. After a moment, I recognized our neighborhood. Familiar buildings whizzed by. Unlike the rest of Tokyo, there were no skyscrapers in this part of town. The streets were narrow and crooked, a throwback to an earlier time when Tokyo was still "Edo."

The motorcycles flew down the narrow streets, staying in remarkably tight formation. Heihachi and I were on the outside of the group, and I was sure that if I extended my arm I could touch the side of the building as we zoomed past. I thought of it momentarily, but I dared not let go of Heihachi as we flew along. I had never moved through our little neighborhood so quickly and was quite disoriented to see it all in such a compressed manner.

Our house was three stories high, but the bottom story was halfway submerged below ground, almost a basement. That gave the house a short stocky feeling and helped it blend in with the neighbors' houses which were only two stories tall and much older than ours. When we moved in the realtor told us that the house was "two and a half stories" because the bottom story was a partial basement. I had teased Ken saying the "half story" would be the perfect size for him because he was short. He had just shrugged it off, as he did so often when I teased him.

The entry way to the house was down a short flight of stone stairs to the semi-submerged level. An ivy plant clung to the exterior of the dwelling above the entry way, softening the view and giving the place what I thought to be a warm, homey feeling.

Inside the house, a staircase brought one up to the next story, then more stairs to the second floor, where our bedrooms were located.

The lot the house was built on was "L" shaped, and only a very narrow section was exposed to the street, as if the house wanted to avoid calling attention to itself. After visiting the Palace, all of the houses in our neighborhood looked defenseless and small. Our shy little house, half sunken into the ground, was the smallest of the bunch. Unlike the Palace, there were no high walls around the perimeter. No gates. No moat. I didn't know how we were going to defend it.

I sighed at the hopelessness of our situation. Before I could give it another thought, however, I heard Kanbei's voice in my ear.

"Let's park the bikes here and go in on foot." He pointed at a small parking area a short walk from our house.

Moving in tandem, the motorcycles abruptly veered into the parking lot Kanbei had indicated and came to a halt. The samurai killed their engines, and the roar of the trip gave way to the quiet sounds of our little neighborhood. I slid off the seat behind Heihachi and planted my feet in front of the inky black motorcycle, a bit wobbly from the speed and motion of the trip. Pulling off my helmet, I heard the familiar sounds of Hatsudai.

It had only been a day since we had left, but so much had happened since then that I felt oddly disoriented. The idea of 'normal' seemed far away, like a dream that is hard to remember.

"Heihachi, the map," Kanbei said and Heihachi immediately pulled out a wafer-thin computer, handing it to Kanbei. I had never seen anything like it. The computer was almost transparent, and the screen immediately came to life in Kanbei's hands. A map of the area floated above the surface of the screen.

"They will most likely come from here," Kanbei said, pointing to a patch of green on the map.

I noticed that as we got closer to the fight Kanbei got less and less polite. It wasn't that he was rude. He just had less time to spend on pleasantries, and his orders became more direct. His brevity added to the sense of urgency we all felt about the upcoming battle.

When Kanbei finished his strategic review of the map, we walked the short distance to our house. If Kanbei had the same sense of hopelessness at the thought of defending this little place as I had, he didn't show it. He walked confidently ahead of the group.

As we approached Emvee came out to meet us. He pranced about, clearly happy to see us. His tail which curled up over his back wagged at the sight of us.

"It is just our dog," Ken explained. "He doesn't like anybody. But don't worry. His bark is worse than his bite..."

His voice trailed off because Emvee had gone up to Heihachi and was licking his hand. The two were carrying on as if they were old friends.

"Wow, that's weird," I said. "He never likes strangers."

Emvee crouched down low with his tail section high in the air. His curlicue tail wagged vigorously, inviting Heihachi to chase him.

I wondered why Emvee was being so friendly to the samurai.

"Have you guys ever seen our dog before?" I asked, a cross between curiosity and suspicion.

"Uh..." Heihachi had a guilty look on his face and his eyes darted quickly to Kanbei.

"We thought a dog would be of value to you," said Kanbei.

"You gave us this dog?" I asked incredulously. That explained how the dog mysteriously showed up on our doorstep.

How had they picked us? What kind of dog was this that they had given us? How had the chosen us as the recipients? My mind was filled with questions, but before I could ask them Kanbei cut me off. "We should prepare. We might not have much time."

We spent the rest of the day prepping the house for an onslaught of monsters. Dad was at the office, and we had the place to ourselves. Katsushiro and Kyuzo busied themselves putting shutters over the windows. Heihachi followed closely behind them, carefully writing kanji characters on the shuttered windows. I could not read what he had written.

"What is that?" Ken asked, pointing at the rows of neatly inked characters.

"Deters the blue *oni*. They don't like those," Heihachi said casually.

"Like a spell?" Ken asked.

"Spell? Yeah, spell. Prayer. Something like that," Heihachi said with a shrug. His nonchalant attitude contrasted with the meticulous work he was doing with the brush in his hand.

Ken looked at me with an unspoken question written on his face. I turned my palms up and shrugged in response. We had no idea why kanji characters painted on the shutters would deter the lethal blue monsters.

Heihachi caught us looking at other and said, "Words have power. More power than you know. And these words are particularly powerful. Keep *oni* out."

The plan was to divert the blue *oni* away from the shuttered windows and attract them to where we wanted them to enter the house. Heihachi told us he didn't believe the kanji characters were foolproof, but his hope was that they would be enough to divert the *oni*.

For Ken's benefit he drew a smiley face on one of the shutters and wrote under it "have a nice day." Ken laughed.

Inside the house, Kyuzo moved furniture. He piled tables and chairs into the kitchen, clearing the living room.

"We need space to fight," he told me quietly, then went back to his work with stony-faced determination.

Somehow Heihachi had found a schematic diagram of our house and loaded it onto Kanbei's impossibly thin tablet. Kanbei poured over the layout as he walked through the house. He decided that we would open the door on the second-floor balcony. We hoped that the *oni* would come through that door and we could fight with them in the narrow halls and on the stairs to the living room.

"How can we fight them more easily?" Kanbei asked Heihachi. Even Kanbei deferred to Heihachi's knowledge of the monsters.

"Fight them in a tight space. The lack of maneuverability will work to our advantage."

"Fight them close in," Kyuzo said nodding. It made sense to him. His emotionless stare changed for just a moment. It was the closest thing to a smile I had seen on his face. I thought he was imagining a sword fight with the *oni*.

The stairs from the second floor led to a long hallway. Katsushiro flipped one of the tables that Kyuzo had moved and made a fort. He lined up his arrows and set his bow behind the table. Then perching himself on the nearby sofa, Katsushiro examined his setup. His arrows were carefully aligned and his bow was in easy reach. He leaned back in the sofa and looked very comfortable for a moment.

Just at then, Heihachi entered the room and found Katsushiro leaning back on the couch. He began to tease the younger samurai.

"Can I get you anything? Bring you something to drink perhaps? Hmmm?"

Katsushiro shot back, "Yes, would you get me a double decaf skinny latte, if it isn't too much trouble?"

They both laughed good-naturedly.

The samurai were much more at ease than I felt. I wondered if one gets comfortable with the thought of death. Perhaps they had faced death so often that it no longer bothered them. Here they were laughing with each other. I, on the other hand, couldn't stop thinking about the blue *oni* and the danger that we faced.

A single *oni* had practically killed me and my brother. Katsushiro and Kanbei had battled the monster to a draw. Now we were expecting – should I even say "hoping for"? – the arrival of an entire clan of *oni*. Whatever that meant. Seven? Eight *oni*? The odds of us living through the night were pretty small. I thought for sure we were faced with certain death, but the samurai were joking with each other, seemingly at ease.

I listened to their good-humored conversation with a grim look on my face.

Kanbei interrupted my thoughts.

"Okay. Let's go. We will meet upstairs to review the battle plan."

We all filed upstairs.

"Maya, you will wait on the balcony as long as possible. The blue *oni* will be attracted to your scent. After that you will drop back into the house and retreat downstairs. We want to let them in."

Kanbei did not patronize me. He did not suggest that I should be treated differently because of my age or because I was a girl. He just outlined the battle plan to all of us with a realistic assessment of our skills.

"As the monsters come through the house we will try to kill as many as possible." His voice was confident giving orders.

"Katsushiro, you have your watch in the living room on the first floor. Use your arrows to stop as many as possible. Heihachi, you are with Katsushiro. Remember the fewer that get past you, the fewer we have to fight," the older samurai instructed. "Kyuzo, you wait in this room and finish the rest. You are the final defense before the safe room, where Ken and Maya are."

"The blue *oni* will probably be after her. In all likelihood they will not be focused on you. I don't have to tell you how important it is that none of the monsters gets their hands on Maya. Ken, you are our last defense. All right, that's it. Keep your eyes open and your hands on your sword hilts."

We moved into our positions to wait for the onslaught of blue *oni*. My feet were heavy as I went to the second floor to take my place on the balcony. Outside, the sun was setting behind the house and the sky in front of me was already growing dark and the temperature was dropping. A few stars were visible in the twilight sky, winking at me from the safety of their distant positions. It had been a busy day and time had flown by quickly. I realized, however, I missed the vanishing sunlight. The growing darkness made me anxious. My stomach did flip flops, and images of blue talons flickered through my mind.

Waiting for the attack, everything in the house was quiet. Eerily quiet. Suddenly I heard something from the hall downstairs. It was a scraping sound at the door. It stopped, and everything was quiet again. We waited silently from our position on the second floor, listening carefully for the sound of the monster approaching.

There it was again.

It was just barely audible. My heart froze. It was a faint scraping at the door. Gently. Persistently. It was coming from the front door downstairs. I held my breath.

Whoever it was – whatever it was – hadn't bothered to knock or ring the doorbell.

"They are here," I mouthed the words to Kanbei. He nodded, then motioned for me to go to my hiding place downstairs. He quietly pulled his sword out in one fluid motion and came down the stairs behind me. We walked in absolute silence. Why hadn't the monsters come in through the balcony as we had hoped?

Noiselessly we crept down the stairs. As quietly as possible I followed the narrow hallway to the front door of the home.

Scratch-scratch.

There it was again. Just outside the door. Like metal on metal. I imagined a dirty talon on the door knob.

Everything was quiet again. I moved to follow Kanbei. As we crept silently towards the door, my scabbard brushed against the wall of the hallway. It barely made a sound, but in the silence the small noise rang loud in our ears. Everyone froze. Kanbei turned to look. I cringed. Had I given us away? To my relief his look was not reproachful.

"Sorry," I mouthed the word silently. Kanbei nodded, and we continued creeping forward. Everything was quiet.

Behind us, Katsushiro slipped silently over the table and put an arrow into his bow. He pulled the string back. The bow creaked as he stretched the arrow back. It was the only sound in the house. We all glanced his way at the sound. The bow was tight and ready to explode its arrow out into the monster.

We waited in front of the door. I breathed out slowly. We were as ready for the attack as we could be.

With a sword in one hand, Kanbei reached for the door knob. He would open it and swing the sword on the monster outside. Slowly...

Suddenly the front door flew open. In through the doorway came my father.

"Dad!" Ken and I said in unison.

"I got home early," he said distractedly, putting his briefcase down in the doorway and coming into the room. He hadn't noticed the others in the room.

"Wow. I can't believe how cold it is out. I thought we could make some hot choc..choc..." His words trailed off as he saw the four samurai standing in the room with swords drawn and arrows at the ready.

"...chocolate," he finished quietly.

"Dad, I want you to meet the samurai who are here to save my life," I said.

"Awkward," Heihachi whispered quietly under his breath to Ken and stuck his sword into its scabbard.

"Uh, hello..." Dad said, regarding the strangers in our house with wary eyes.

"Dad, it's like I told you on the phone," Ken jumped in. "Maya was attacked by an *oni* at a shrine..."

"Blue *oni*," Heihachi interjected.

"Right. Blue *oni* at a shrine," Ken continued, "And these guys saved us. They took us to the Emperor's Palace and now they are going to help protect us."

"What?" Dad asked, looking more stunned than anything else.

"They're samurai. Here to protect us," Ken tried again.

"I thought that was some kind of video game you were playing," Dad said.

"I assure you this is not a game, Donovan-sama. The danger is very real," Kanbei said.

"What's an *oni* anyway?" Dad asked.

"Blue *oni*," Heihachi corrected again.

"What's a blue *oni*?" Dad asked again.

"Japanese troll," Katsushiro answered.

The other samurai put their swords back in their *saya*.

"Sir, I know this must come as a shock to you," Kanbei explained quickly to my father. "But there isn't much time. We have to prepare. A clan of Japanese *oni* will attack here very soon and we must get ready. Your daughter's life is at stake."

"My daughter..." my Dad's voice trailed off. He thought for a moment, trying to take it all in. Or remembering something. I wondered what would happen if my father asked the samurai to leave. I really couldn't blame him if he didn't believe them. After all that we had seen, I could barely believe it myself. My father had seen a bunch of strange samurai standing in his house, armed to the teeth. It wouldn't be weird if he just asked them to leave and sent us to our rooms. I wondered what would happen to us if the blue *oni* attacked without the samurai's protection. I shuddered. Thoughts of hardened blue skin and daunting yellow eyes made me very uneasy. It raised the hairs on the back of my neck.

"Sir, this is what their mother would want," Heihachi said.

I thought it was an odd comment, but the mention of my mother seemed to galvanize Dad's will. He straightened his shoulders. Looking Kanbei in the eye, he nodded.

"Okay. You have my support. What can I do?" he said quietly.

"Here," Kyuzo said and gave my dad a short sword that he was carrying. "Use this."

Dad took the blade in his hand and looked at it. "Okay, I can do this."

"He hasn't had the training," Heihachi said.

"There isn't time," Kanbei said. "He will have to fight the best he can."

"Mr. Donovan, you should stay in this room with your son. We have reason to believe that the *oni* will be after her primarily."

"Okay, let's get ready," Kanbei said. "To your posts. Maya come with me. We will have you wait on the balcony."

"What? The balcony?" Dad said, panicking.

"I thought you said we were trying to protect her."

"We need the blue *oni* to come in close if we are to fight them effectively," Heihachi answered matter-of-factly. "We need to draw them into the house."

"No. No way. We can't just put her outside. If these things are as dangerous as you say they are..."

"Dad, please. I'll be okay," I told my father. I looked into his eyes. He stared back at me.

"I don't want anything to happen to you," he said softly.

"I know. I'll be fine," I assured him. I tried to make my voice sound more confident than I actually felt.

My father's shoulders shifted slightly and the muscles in his neck stiffened. In that moment I saw something new.  It was the type of observation that I had when we had been practicing at the Imperial Palace. It felt like the tea-induced awareness, but the effects of the tea and the heightened sensitivity were long since out of my blood stream.  In that instant I saw in my father something I had not seen before. What could it be?  It flickered across his face, only lasting a moment.  The answer hit me like a ton of bricks.  It was fear.  How could I have been so dense?  It was the fear of losing me.

His breathing changed, and I sensed the loss that he had felt when he lost Mom. I saw it in his expression. I could read it like a book. I saw in his eyes the depth of his love for her – and now his love for us. It wasn't that I was able to read his mind, but in some way, I was able to intuit his feelings.  I saw in his face that he was thinking about Mom.  It was as if my eyes were opened, and I was seeing him for the first time.

"Oh," I said, although I wasn't sure if I said it out loud.  I could feel the emotion rising up in me.

Katsushiro was watching me carefully.  All too often he knew what was going on in my head, but I was not sure if he could read me this time.  Did he know what I had seen in my father's heart?  He smiled at me and turned back towards my father.

"At the first sign of the *oni* we will send her into the house.  We will protect her," Kanbei sounded confident enough for both of us.

"It's going to be alright, Dad," I said, giving him a quick hug. "I'm going to be okay."

Eventually, Dad relented and went with Ken, while I returned upstairs with Kanbei and Heihachi.  Katsushiro and Kyuzo got into their positions as well, and we all settled in for a long wait.

The house became very quiet.

"The blue *oni* will begin to move at sunset," Heihachi had said. "And at midnight they will finish their rituals. We can expect them some time after that."

I looked at my watch. It was 12:05.  My palms were sweaty. I wiped them on my pants and then put my hand on the handle of my sword. I wondered what kind of horrific rituals those monsters performed and tried to calm my breathing.

"Wearing a sword," Kyuzo had said in our training, "Is an outward expression of the samurai's preparedness in all circumstances." I tried to tell myself that I was ready for the battle I was about to face.

Suddenly the quiet was broken by a sound outside. We all froze in our tracks. Was it the *oni*? After a moment that seemed like forever, I heard a sound I recognized. It was Emvee. We had left him outside! He was barking.

"We have to get him!" I said and raced downstairs.

"No! It is too dangerous!" Kanbei yelled. Ignoring him, I ran out of the room.

"We have to save him," I said more to myself than to anyone else. I got downstairs, but Katsushiro was there. He grabbed me, holding me tightly in his arms. I tried to shake loose.

"No, I have to get him. The *oni* will kill him," I said. I was frantic. I struggled to get free but Katsushiro held me tightly.

Dad and Ken watched me without moving. Suddenly something in Dad's face changed. He pulled the short sword that Kyuzo had given him out of its scabbard and ran to the entry way. He unlocked the door and threw it open. A burst of cold air blew into the room.

"No wait! It is too dangerous," Kanbei yelled. He had followed me downstairs. It was too late. Dad was already outside. I could hear him calling for Emvee.

Everything went silent. We waited. I looked at Ken anxiously. From my position in the entryway, I could see the yard where Emvee should be. How had he gotten off his leash? I could no longer hear my father who had been calling for the dog. I worried that something had happened to both of them. Horrible half-fashioned images of a blue *oni* flashed through my mind.

"Dad?" I called, my voice filled with worry.

Waiting nervously, I looked at the painting hanging in our entryway. It was a hunting scene. Several dogs ferociously attacked two evil looking bears. I had always liked that painting, but I had always worried about the safety of the dogs. The bears had sharp claws and were growling fiercely. The dogs, however, were undaunted. The artist had captured their courage. Now I couldn't help but think of *oni* when I looked at it.

I turned to look at Ken who was frozen in his spot in by the door. Suddenly, the door swung open and Dad came back in. He was carrying Emvee in his arms.

"Dad! Emvee!" I shouted and ran to them in great relief.

Ken slammed the door and locked it behind them as they came in.

"That was very dangerous," Kanbei said. He was worried I could tell. "You must not risk your life like that. Your children need you!"

He checked the door to be sure that it was locked, and then when he was sure that it was safe, he put his sword back into its *saya*.

"These guys aren't the only ones who can be brave," Dad said to us, as he set the dog down on the floor.

Emvee was excited to be back in the house. He dropped into a playful position, his tail curled up behind him. He barked a challenge, wanting to play. I was so relieved that he was safe.

"Okay everyone back to your posts," Kanbei finally ordered us. He was clearly disappointed with our lack of discipline, but he was relieved that we were okay. He wasn't the type to stay mad very long.

Feeling a bit guilty but relieved to have Emvee back, I went back upstairs to wait for the blue *oni* to attack. Ken followed me to keep me company. Dad returned to the den, our safe room.

"I'm worried, Ken," I confessed when we were alone. Something painful was going on in my head. My arm throbbed where the *oni* had licked me. The feeling was strong and getting worse.

"About?"

"I'm not sure I can do this."

"Fight the *oni*?"

"Mmm," I nodded. A feeling of helplessness overwhelmed me. The *oni's* poison was coursing through me, amplifying my worst fears. It was in my blood. Although I didn't know it at the time, I felt out of sorts and could tell something was wrong. "It's more than I'm capable of."

"Do you want to quit?" he asked me.

"I never should have brought you into this," I said. "It's too dangerous for you."

"No, Maya. I chose to come with you. We all chose to be here, to help you with this."

He was so brave. I felt so afraid. In a flash, I hated him for it. More *oni* poison twisting my brain. In my head I fought back. "You don't hate your brother, Maya." I couldn't give in to my dark feelings.

I knew the *oni* was the problem, not my brother, but it was hard to resist the swelling anger running through my veins. At the time, I didn't understand the chemical basis for my emotions. I was infected but didn't know it. I knew, however, that the *oni* was to blame. And the only solution was to destroy it. I knew what we had to do, but I wasn't sure if our plan was going to work. My insides had turned to ice, and I was desperately worried about Ken. Now Dad was at risk too. I felt like I was going to cry. Again. Once again, my emotions were out of control. I got angry with myself which only made it worse.

"Oh, Maya," Ken said, and he put his hand on my arm. He was quiet for a moment then, "I don't know what to say. I know you can do this."

"Yeah?" I sniffed, looking up at him. He nodded. I wiped my eyes, trying to get a grip on my feelings. "I just wished none of this had ever happened to me. I wish we had never met that stupid *oni*."

"Blue *oni*," Ken corrected me, sounding like one of the samurai. It made me smile.

"Blue *oni*. I wish it had never happened and we were just normal kids again, thinking about school."

"I don't know why this happened to us, Maya," Ken said. "But I know you can do it."

He paused, looking at me. At the time, I thought that it was nerves and self-doubt, but it was plaguing me. Ken saw this in me and his tone changed. Now he was teasing.

"Besides," he said, "Do you want to live forever?" He raised one eyebrow.

"YOLO, baby," I said, laughing and crying at the same time. I was thinking of all the times Ken and I had said that word before. It was the punch line to a joke for us. The word that I would say before I would eat an Oreo. The word that Ken said before he launched his bike off of a hill. Or when he grabbed his skateboard to go outside and play.

In this context it was a sweet reminder of a life that I had almost forgotten. Now the idea that life was short was all too real to me. I realized that Ken and I might not make it through the night.

"Stupid blue *oni*," I said.

Ken was so brave, and I admired him for helping me. I sniffed and dried my tears. I gave him a quick hug. Our armor made a dull *thunk* when we hugged.

"You'd better get back to your post or you're going to get busted," I told him, trying to sound like an older sister.

"You got it, Maya," he said and gave me a mock salute. He disappeared downstairs, and we both settled in to wait for the attack.

## Chapter Seven
### The Battle of Hatsudai

Hours passed, but the *oni* did not arrive. Everything was dark. Darker, in fact, than it had been all night. There was no moon. No lights were in the sky. A tomb-like darkness had swallowed up all the light.

To make matters worse, Kanbei had ordered us to douse the lights in the house. No lights. No sounds. Just waiting.

In the darkness, there was something else. Something was pressing on me. The night air had a thickness to it. It was heavy and threatening, as if something had settled in. I could feel it – maybe we all could – but for me it was overpowering. I couldn't relax, couldn't settle my nerves.

"Evil is about to swallow the world in blackness," I whispered, more to myself than to anyone else.

Above all, I wanted to run. I wanted to get away, but I knew there was no place to escape for me now. I had to force myself to stay in one room.

Pacing nervously, I fingered the hilt of my sword, careful not to unsheathe it. I did not want to use it. Not then. Not ever. I didn't want to pull it from its scabbard. I was afraid of the weapon, afraid of what it could do. I almost believed that the sword had a mind of its own. That it was capable of something terrible without me, and it made me afraid.

There is no way I could have known it, but the poison of the blue *oni* had taken over my body. My nerves were a wreck, and it was only getting worse.

Heihachi watched me with a curious look as I paced and then walked softly to where Kanbei was waiting. I heard them whispering quietly in Japanese, and Kanbei looked over at me. I couldn't understand what they were saying, but I assumed that Heihachi was asking the questions and Kanbei was offering instructions. I was wrong.

They both returned to the place where I was waiting. Kanbei made a gesture with his hand, summoning Katsushiro and Kyuzo who silently emerged from the shadows to join us.

Katsushiro smiled at me briefly as he approached. I know he meant it as a "hey-buck-up-it'll-all-be-okay" smile, but I was in desperate need of support and soaked up his attention greedily. I looked into his eyes. I let my gaze linger on his cheeks, on his strong jaw. He must have caught the expression on my face, because his eyes locked on mine and his face changed. The moment lasted for an instant before I was jerked back to the reality of the moment.

Kanbei missed it, or if he caught it, he said nothing. He began speaking in a hushed tone. "We cannot wait for them to find us. We need to draw them in."

"Draw them in?" I asked. Kanbei nodded. "Draw them in where?"

Kanbei didn't respond to me but looked to the other samurai.

"What are you suggesting? I thought we were going to wait," I whispered.

Kanbei held up something in the darkness. I squinted at the dark shape. It was my 'I heart Tokyo' t-shirt. He must have picked it up at the Palace. It was in shreds after the attack by the *maneki-neko* and dangled limply in his hand.

"It is very dangerous," Katsushiro said, understanding Kanbei's meaning.

I shook my head, still not picking up on his drift. "What are you talking about?"

I looked at Heihachi, who turned away from me, his face visibly paler in the darkness. What had he done?

"I will go," Kyuzo volunteered.

Kanbei paused to think about it for a moment. I looked from one samurai to the next, trying to put the pieces together.

"Take this," Kanbei said and gave Kyuzo my shirt. He handled it carefully.

Turning to me, Katsushiro explained quietly, "The shirt has your scent. The *oni* will surely pick it up."

"Wait. What?" I asked, my eyes wide with horror finally understanding what was happening. I knew my voice was too loud. "He's going into their nest?"

"Not in but close. He will plant the scent and try to draw them to us."

"But they're coming here. We are waiting for them to come here," I protested. My voice was louder than it should have been, but this was crazy. It was too dangerous. How could Kanbei suggest it?

Without another word Kyuzo carefully folded my shirt and tucked it into his belt. It created a lump which he smoothed carefully with his hand. Then he turned on his heel and walked out of the room.

"Wait. No!" I yelled, but it was too late. He was out of the room and down the stairs to the door. He walked silently, making no noise as he left.

"It's not supposed to happen this way," I protested, turning from Kanbei to Katsushiro. "The plan was that we would wait here. We are waiting for them. He can't go. It's too dangerous. He'll be killed!"

I couldn't bear to think of Kyuzo going out into the black night alone. Not with those horrible blue *oni* out there. I knew they were out there. I could feel it. I glared at the samurai, but their eyes met mine with no emotion. It was a dangerous task, but one that had to be done, and Kyuzo had volunteered to do it. Seeing the issue was settled in their minds, I reluctantly returned to my post.

I sat alone, brooding. What would make a man live on the edge of death like this? Kyuzo was so willing to face evil. He was calm as he left, steady. I thought I might never see him again and wished I had said something to him before he left. It was too late now. He was out of the house and well on his way. I knew he was facing overwhelming odds, but he had not flinched. Life felt very different from the movies.

Anxiously, I settled in to wait, thinking angry thoughts about Kanbei and Katsushiro. Why did they let him go? I sank to the floor in the now furniture-less room and leaned against the wall, placing my *katana* on the ground in front of me. I crossed my arms around my legs and rested my head on my knees.

I thought about Kyuzo making his way alone to where the *oni* were gathered. Just thinking about it made my palms sweat. Would he return? I thought of Heihachi who had been knocked out and taken into the blue *oni's* lair. I hated to dwell on unpleasant thoughts, but I couldn't help but wonder what those *oni* had planned for Heihachi had he not gotten away. Would they have pulled him apart? Swiftly bitten off his head? Would it have been by a single *oni*? Or several at the same time? Would he be food for the monsters? Or would they just kill him from spite?

"Those are terrible thoughts, Maya," I said out loud with some measure of self-reproach. "Think of something positive."

My thoughts drifted to an early happy memory. It was a Sunday morning many years ago and my father and mother were still asleep in their room. In those early days, Ken and I had willingly shared a room, and because we were both up early, we had determined to sneak downstairs and wake my parents. The pink light of the early morning splashed through the window and spilled onto the covers of their bed as Ken and I snuck giggling into their room. We were still dressed in our pajamas. We knelt down and waddled alongside the bed, preparing to surprise them. Brimming with childish glee, I poked my head up above the horizon of the bed and found the mound of blankets that must be my father's sleeping form. With the drama of an illusionist performing some great magical trick, I pulled the covers off of my father. To my horror, I saw that lying between my father and my mother was the same frightening blue *oni* that had tried to eat me in the shrine the day before.

"Run, Ken," I screamed, turning to see him escape to safety in a blur behind me. I turned back to face the *oni*. On the far side of the bed, my mom slipped over the edge and melted out of view the way people sometimes do in dreams. The *oni* grabbed my father in one hand and rested a sharp claw at the base of my father's neck.

"No!" I opened my mouth to scream, but no words came out.

I saw my father's body slump, then suddenly, the *oni* was unspeakably close to my face, snapping its teeth at me. Terrified, I tried to run away, but the *oni* towered over me like the angel of death. I tried to run, but I couldn't move. My feet were glued to the floor. I couldn't get away. The monster came towards me, radiating evil. It came closer and closer. Again, I tried to scream, but I could not.

"Maya?" Katsushiro asked gently. I had fallen asleep. I awoke with a start at Katsushiro's gentle touch on my shoulder. Breathing heavily, I struggled to get my bearings, looking around with confusion. Katsushiro was close to me, a gentle look on his face.

"I was dreaming," I said at last. Once again Katsushiro had saved me.

"You called out in your sleep," he said, sitting on the floor beside me. I felt terrible for falling asleep, but there was no reproach in his voice. He was not angry.

"It was terrible," I said. "I couldn't get away. I couldn't fight back."

"You're okay now."

"It was such a terrible dream."

"You're fine. It's okay."

"I think I'm going crazy."

"Sometimes the biggest enemy of self is self," Katsushiro said quietly. He cocked his head and looked at me. I studied his face. His angular cheeks stood out in the dim light of the room. Katsushiro. I wanted to throw my arms around him. I was starving for protection, and Katsushiro's embrace was the safest place I could think of.

"I'm afraid," I confessed to him. He nodded. "It must seem ridiculous to you. You're a samurai."

"It's the blue *oni*," he explained. "Their presence darkens the heart."

He clenched his jaw and tightened his grip on the hilt of his sword. I wondered if he felt the presence of the blue *oni* as well. We sat there for a moment, shoulder to shoulder, leaning our backs against the wall, staring out at the dark room. My thoughts drifted to Kyuzo.

"He'll probably be back soon," I said, looking over at Katsushiro anxiously and hoping he'd corroborate my story.

"Yes, he probably will."

I felt grateful for his willingness to help. He had told me what I wanted to hear. Now there was nothing more to say. I shifted my weight against the wall in the dark and listened for any sound in the house. It was utterly quiet. I became aware of Katsushiro breathing softly beside me.

We sat there for a moment longer not saying anything – just breathing – until I made a show of checking my watch. I could just locate it under the armor on my arm. I pulled it down on my wrist, shifting my armor up. Hours had gone by. No sign of blue *oni*. And no sign of Kyuzo.

"Look at the time," I said. Katsushiro nodded, not really looking at the watch. "I'd better go check on Ken."

I pushed myself up and walked out, leaving Katsushiro still sitting with his back against the wall.

As quietly as I could, I went downstairs to check on Ken. Passing through the living room, I nodded at Heihachi and Kanbei who were waiting in the living room patiently. They nodded to me as I passed. Descending the last flight of stairs to the half basement, I found Ken. He was snuggled next to Dad in the den, both of them barely awake.

"Hey kid. Come here," Dad said, sitting up and gesturing at the sofa next to him. "Have a seat."

"Everything okay down here?" I asked, making myself comfortable next to Ken who was barely awake.

"Yeah. You?"

"I think so," I said, getting comfy on the sofa. If we weren't waiting for blue *oni* to overrun the house, it would have felt like an average movie night. "I'm worried about Kyuzo," I confessed.

"Don't worry about them. These samurai know how to take care of themselves."

"How do you know that?" I asked.

"Know what?"

"How do you know about the samurai?"

Dad took a deep breath. The dim light from a distant streetlight crept through the window and lit his face from one side.

"Pumpkin, there is something I never told you." His voice took on a faraway quality. He was talking to me but his thoughts were somewhere else.

"Mm?"

"It's about your mom," he said. Even in the dim light I could see that his eyes were staring into the distance. "Your mom..." His voice trailed off. Dad never talked about Mom. Sitting next to us, Ken caught it too and sat up a little, pulling himself out of sleep to listen to the conversation.

"It's about Mom?" I asked and frowned. Dad nodded. "What about her?"

"When she left... she uh... she left to become a samurai."

"What? That's great," I said not thinking carefully. "Maybe they can help us find her."

"No."

"Sure. Maybe. We won't know unless we ask. Maybe they'll know where she is." I couldn't believe what he was saying, and my only thought was that maybe we could meet her. Kanbei would know how to contact her.

"Maya, no."

"Why not? They must have some records on these things."

"Look," he said visibly upset. "She's gone. She died. She died because of the samurai." I could tell it was hard for him to talk this way.

"What?"

"That's why we left Japan. We had to leave. I had to leave. It was too hard to stay."

"Wait, our mom was with the samurai?" Ken asked. My father nodded. I remember the shocked look on Ken's face and knew I must have the same expression on my face. Nothing my father was saying was making sense to me.

"How did she die?"

"I wasn't there. I couldn't help her."

"How did it happen?"

"I don't know. I thought the samurai were going to protect her. They said they were going to protect her. That's what she said. That's what they told me." He shook his head, emotion welling up in him. "But they couldn't save her. They couldn't protect her. Nobody could."

"Dad, this is so weird. You're saying you've known about these samurai all along? Why didn't you tell us something?" I got up off the sofa. I was agitated and needed to move.

"What happened to Mom?" Ken asked.

"You don't understand. You both don't understand. There are things out there, things that are so evil..." his voice trailed off.

"Why didn't you tell us?" I asked, pacing the floor. I couldn't believe what I was hearing.

"Tell you what? That your mom was savagely attacked by some weird snow monster and never seen again? That's not the kind of thing anyone would believe."

"What happened to her?"

"She was taken by one of the *yokai*."

"But she left with the samurai?"

"The samurai said they were going to protect her. They said they could save her. That's what they said. You can't trust these samurai, Maya. They say they will help you but they won't."

"How can you say that, Dad? They are trying to help us. They risked their lives for us," I said thinking about what had happened in the shrine.

"They are *still* risking their lives for us," Ken said, reminding me that even now Kyuzo was out there alone trying to lure the *oni* back to us.

"But that's why she left? We always thought that she just...left," Ken said. It was true. With no evidence to the contrary, Ken and I made up our own explanations about what had happened to our mother. Because my father had been so unwilling to speak about it, we were left to our own imaginations.

"I'm not sure we can trust these guys, Maya," my father said. "What if they can't protect you?"

"I can't believe you're just telling us this now," I spit out, and with that, I walked out of the den. I could hear my father calling my name, but I needed to be alone and figure things out. My mind was racing with the thought of Mom working together with the samurai. I sat down on the stairs between the two floors, my father in the room with Ken below me and the samurai in the living room upstairs. I wondered if Dad was right. Could I trust the samurai to protect me? In my heart I believed that they were willing to help me, but after what he had said I began to wonder if they were capable. That one blue *oni* in the shrine had practically destroyed us. Now Heihachi said that they were coming in force. I wondered if our plan could ever succeed.

Just then, I heard a sound at the door. It was a slight rattling as something pushed against the outside. I jumped to my feet.

"It's him," I thought and ran to the entryway to unlock it. I don't know why I thought it was him. I just had a feeling. Forgetting all precautions, I threw the door open. It was Kyuzo! He had returned! He entered the house, and I quickly locked the door after him, twisting the deadbolt behind us.

He said nothing as he entered the room. Looking at his face I couldn't tell if the mission had been successful or not. I searched his expression for clues. As usual, he neither smiled nor frowned. His face was a mask of samurai stoicism.

I was so overjoyed to see him back that I wanted to hug him, but I didn't dare. Something about his demeanor held me back. If I could, I would have thrown my arms around him. I was so glad to see him home in one piece. My heart felt like it was going to burst. Kyuzo caught my look, stared at me for a moment then shifted his gaze to the ground. Without saying a word, he pushed past me and went upstairs to report to Kanbei. I followed close behind, eager to hear what had happened.

Kanbei, Katsushiro and Heihachi gathered to welcome Kyuzo back with serious faces. They said nothing but gathered around the returned warrior with expectant faces, waiting for his report.

At last Kyuzo said, "They are coming now. We had better prepare."

"How long?" Kanbei asked.

"Minutes at best. They are close behind."

Kanbei nodded. He looked at the others. It was an unspoken order. Each samurai left for his designated position, silently moving away.

"That's it?" I wondered, holding my ground and feeling reluctant to take up my post. No words of thanks for the man who risked his life for mine? I couldn't believe that we weren't going to at least show our appreciation. This was the first time I had encountered the stoicism of the samurai, but it would not be the last. I looked after Kanbei incredulously, but he was already headed to his post.

Failing to garner support from the other samurai, I turned to follow Kyuzo, determined to show him my gratitude. If no one else was going to thank him for his heroic service, I would. I came up behind him as he was settling into his position. He pulled his *katana* from his belt and leaned it against the wall. Noticing me, he looked up to face me.

"What is it?" he said, raising an eyebrow. His style was abrupt, and it gave me pause. I wasn't sure if I should continue. He was so stern.

"I just wanted to say..." my voice trailed off. I swallowed nervously.

Kyuzo seemed uncomfortable with the attention. He looked around the room, not meeting my gaze. He had risked his life for us – for me – and now it was as if he had forgotten. He shrugged it off as if it were nothing.

"Go on," he said impatiently.

"I just wanted to say," I tried again, stammering for the right words. Nothing came to me. My mind went blank. All I could think of was the swelling of my heart. "I think you are incredible."

A look of surprise crossed his face, then he nodded in acknowledgement. He said nothing but looked around again uncomfortably. I waited for a moment longer, wondering if I should say anything else. Or maybe I was hoping he would say something to me. When I saw that he wasn't going to respond, I turned to go. Just as I was about to leave, out of the corner of my eye, I caught an almost imperceptible smile cross his face.

Feeling like I was going to burst, I ran to my designated spot on the upper floor with Kanbei, taking the stairs two at a time. I slid into the room, slightly out of breath to find him with his back against the wall in the empty room.

I could feel the older samurai's eyes on me as I awkwardly crossed my legs on the floor next to him and turned to see if he was as distracted by the loud beating of my heart as I was. A long pause followed during which I knocked my head gently against the wall behind me and tried unsuccessfully to appear bored. When a sideways glance told me Kanbei's gaze was still on me, I became fascinated by the armor on my wrist, examining it carefully and tracing it slowly with my finger.

Luckily, my sword, which I had positioned against the wall when I sat down, took this moment to slide along the wall and collapse unceremoniously on my head. I returned it to its proper position and resumed my imitation of boredom.

Over the next ten minutes, I caught my breath, and Kanbei's gaze gradually shifted from me. Together we silently peered out of the window towards the postage-stamp-sized balcony. There was nothing to do now but wait. Wait for the inevitable attack. Kyuzo had said they were close.

Outside, snow emerged out of the inky blackness and fell silently on the house, creating a white gauze funeral wrap around the building. It began as small white flakes but as we watched, turned into sticky wet chunks that clung together and covered every horizontal surface. Any other time it would have been beautiful.

I stood up to pace, keeping well clear of the door. The only sound in the house was my feet on the floor. After each step, I paused to listen. Nothing. Another step. Pause. Nothing.

A distant street light cast long shadows across the railing on the balcony and gave the room an eerie glow.

"Where are they?" I whispered to Kanbei. He only looked out the window. He was tense and ready for action.

Cautiously I inched closer to the door to get a better look. Careful not to touch the handle, I peered anxiously through the window out onto the balcony. I could see that the snow had already begun to accumulate. Beyond the balcony, I could make out the neighbor's pale grey house across the street, but it was faint and distant, barely visible now. Seeing nothing on the balcony, I slowly inched back to my waiting spot. I crouched down. Everything was quiet.

Then I heard it.

From the street outside came a low moaning sound. It was a quiet gasp, barely audible, the voice of death calling. I listened carefully, straining to hear it again. I could not tell from which direction it had come.

"How close is it?" I whispered to Kanbei. He shook his head, not daring to speak when the *oni* were this close.

I closed my eyes and saw a tomb open and call my name. A feeling of emptiness clung to me. An ancient menace was here now.

"This is it," I thought. "The *oni* has come for me."

Kanbei eased over to the door and silently turned the handle. It was quiet now. No sound from outside. He gently pushed the door open. It was a glass door on a metal frame with security wire built into the glass itself. It creaked on its hinges as Kanbei opened it, and I froze in my tracks at the noise. I had the horrible feeling that we were being watched.

Noiselessly I moved out into the cold night air in front of Kanbei. The little balcony was still. I tried to imagine what I would see if I looked over the side of the railing at the driveway below. The edge was three or four steps from the safety of the house. To see over that edge, I'd have to walk out onto the balcony. I was terrified, but I made up my mind to look.

Moving as quietly as I could, I stepped out past Kanbei. I slowly inched closer to the edge, leaving him by the glass door. My feet moved without a sound on the rough deck material. First one step. Then a second. Moving towards the edge. The snow, which by now was thick beneath my feet, muffled my steps. Finally, close enough, I could see out over the metal railing. I leaned forward. Slowly. Afraid of what I might see.

Suddenly, I heard a rattling behind me to the right. The noise startled me, and I spun around to look, my heart beating like a drum. It was a rat! A large grey rat had left its nest and was climbing up the rain gutter which ran along the side of our house.

146

It paused to look at me, its nose twitching furiously then scurried up past the balcony towards the roof. Enough adrenaline to get an Olympic team disqualified coursed through my veins. I shivered.

"I hate rats," I said quietly not turning to see if Kanbei was still in the doorway listening to me. I suspected it was going to get a lot worse.

To face the rat, I had turned towards the house, my back to the edge of the balcony. Standing there exposed and vulnerable, I slowly sensed something behind me. It was a dreadful presence that I had experienced before. Something was there now. There was no doubt about it. I could feel it behind me. Holding my breath, I slowly turned my head to look. There it was, just beyond the balcony – a glowing yellow eye in a giant blue face leering back at me. Monstrous. Mesmerizing. The blue *oni* had found me.

The *oni* had managed to climb the outside of the house. I was unprepared for this. I had imagined that the *oni* would stay in the driveway and that the two-and-a-half story height of our house would afford me some measure of safety. Now, however, the *oni* had scaled the outer wall of our home, and its face was eye-level with the railing on the edge of the balcony. No more than a foot or two in front of me, I saw the pale blue horn, which jutted out from above the monster's ear and curved forward, pointing menacingly at me. I was frozen in my tracks, paralyzed by fear.

Out of the corner of my eye, I saw its enormous blue hand quietly appear over the edge of the railing, slowly reaching for me. Long dirty talons extended menacingly from each finger. Even seeing the danger coming closer towards me, I was unable to move. I was frozen in place in front of the giant, the demon.

Everything was just as I had dreamed it and for a moment I was unsure if it was actually happening. So closely did reality resemble the fevered hallucinations I had experienced that I was unable to decide if it was real or not. I was hypnotized by the monster reaching over the railing for me.

I screamed, and when I did, the sound of my own voice broke the spell and startled me into action. My feet felt heavy and unresponsive, but I forced myself to turn around and jump through the doorway. I ran back into the house, past Kanbei who had crept from the doorway and dropped into his hiding spot behind the dresser, silently waiting for the ambush.

If my scream had sent me into motion, it seemed to have had the same effect on the monster as well. The creature leapt over the railing, effortlessly clearing its height and landing on the balcony with a thud. It struggled for a moment to get its enormous frame through the door, but turning its shoulders, it cleared the entry and quickly followed me. With its preternatural speed, it was on me almost immediately.

Downstairs Emvee began to howl.

To my surprise Kanbei did nothing. I could see him in his hiding place behind the dresser, but he did not move. He just crouched there.

"What are you waiting for?" I screamed over my shoulder as I passed him. Kanbei didn't reply.

I ran through the room, headed for the door on the opposite side and then down the stairs as we had practiced. My armor scraped the wall as I careened down along the stairwell. The *oni* charged after me through the upstairs room with blinding speed.

"Do it!" I yelled. Still no reply. Why wasn't he attacking?

Skipping stairs, I made it to the living room, the blue *oni* in close pursuit. I could hear its angry snarls behind me as I got to the bottom of the first flight of stairs. I'd have to clear the living room and then one more flight of stairs in order to get to my safety spot on the floor below me.

Rounding the corner and entering the living room I could feel the monster behind me. It would easily have caught me in an open area, but it was having trouble navigating the narrow hallways of our house. That split-second edge was what I needed to stay ahead of it.

Suddenly an arrow whizzed by my head. I felt the breeze as it passed and saw the blur of the shaft. It was from Katsushiro who was in his spot on the sofa. Confused, I imagined for a moment that it was intended for me. I slowed my pace.

I caught a glimpse of Katsushiro's face in that moment. His young features were contorted into an angry scowl. The presence of these walking evil creatures had a powerful effect on him, and he channeled his anger into his weapon.

"Run, Maya. Run," he yelled.

I picked up the pace as I turned from the living room to start down the stairs towards my hiding place, but as I turned, I caught sight of the *oni* behind me. Katsushiro's arrow had found its mark in the eye socket of the monster. The creature stopped mid-step and reached a hulking blue hand to its face unable to grasp the arrow protruding out of its now blind eye. Disoriented, the creature fell sideways with a gurgling sound, extending its free hand to break its own fall.

Heihachi, who had been waiting impatiently to the side of Katsushiro, was on top of the monster immediately, sword drawn. With both hands on the hilt he used the long blade of his *tachi* to slash the monster's gut. The room was filled with the nauseating smell of *oni* bowels that spilled onto the floor. I started to gag and thought I was going to vomit. A long hiss escaped the creature's mouth as the *oni* took its last breath and slumped to the ground in a meaty heap.

With a practiced motion, Heihachi shook the blood off his sword.

"Have a nice day," he said quietly.

We had succeeded! We had lured the *oni* into our trap, and the samurai had remained hidden, until they ambushed the evil monster. Our plan had worked! Like some video game played to completion, we had killed the *oni*.

"That's it," I thought to myself with a thrill. "I'm safe now."

Triumphantly, I ran back upstairs. Surprisingly, Kanbei was still in hiding behind the dresser. He motioned silently towards the door which was now closed. He must have shut it earlier to seal off any chance of escape for the *oni*.

Emboldened, I strode past him, threw open the door, and ran outside. The snow was thicker now and had already erased all trace of the *oni's* footprints on the balcony. I felt it crunch under my feet. With a feeling of triumph, I looked over the edge of the railing. What I saw made my blood run cold. Ten *oni* were in the driveway below, each seemingly larger than the last. They moved silently, jostling one another like a basket of snakes. The driveway was alive with the swirling form of blue *oni*. I gasped. Hearing the sound, one looked up at me on the balcony with a jaundiced yellow eye. It made a grunting noise – a low guttural noise – and the others turned to eye me with a dreadful glare. It was a terrible feeling, sensing their hateful gaze locked on me.

I don't know why I did what I did next. Maybe it was the adrenaline, derived from seeing the previous *oni* destroyed. Maybe it was confidence in our samurai skills – not my skills, of course, but the skills of the people with me. Truthfully, I just did it without thinking. I jumped up on the low wall of the balcony to look down on the blue *oni*. Standing precariously perched on the edge looking down at the *oni* below, I towered over the awful creatures on the street. One slip and I'd fall the two and half stories into the middle of the angry *oni* mob. I was disgusted by these evil creatures.

"You looking at me?  Are you looking at me?" I shouted as loud as I could, spitting down on them.  All of the monsters froze in their positions and focused on me now.  Like some wild animal when they see prey, the *oni* fixed their gaze on me.  I took off the armored cuff that I wore on my right arm and threw it at one of the *oni* bellow. "I am not going down like some gazelle," I thought. It hit the largest one right in the face.  The cuff was heavy but did no damage to the massive *oni*. However, it did get the monster's attention. It bellowed in rage.

"Bulls eye!" I yelled triumphantly, shaking my fist.

My feeling of victory was short-lived.  In the blink of an eye the *oni* I hit was on the wall of the house coming straight up at me. It had seen me, and it was angry. Long talons sunk into the brick and into the ivy that clung to the exterior of our house.  Headed directly for me, it stared at me intently like some cats do when they see prey.  I heard a low phlegmy growl come from its throat as it easily pulled itself up to the balcony, sending a shower of leaves and broken pieces of wall falling to the ground below.

Immediately fearful, I jumped down backwards off of the railing onto the snow-covered balcony. "Maybe I am like a gazelle," I corrected.  Pivoting on one foot, I turned and ran inside, leaning into my sprint and driving as fast as I could into the house.

"Are more coming?" Kanbei whispered. He hadn't seen all of the monsters writhing in the driveway.

"Oh yeah," I said as I flew past him and poured myself down the stairs as fast as I could.

The commotion rattled the house as one *oni* after another scaled the outside wall, clambering after me.  As I turned the corner and sprinted through the living room, Katsushiro launched another volley of arrows.  Without looking, I knew the monster was close behind me.  Katsushiro had been right.  The *oni* radiated an evil presence that I could actually feel.  The arrows whizzed by with samurai precision.  I heard the twang of the bow and then heard the *oni* snarling in pain behind me.

Upstairs Kanbei came out of hiding and sealed off the escape for the *oni*.  Heihachi and Kyuzo threw themselves into the fight as well.  The house shook with the ferocity of the battle.  And above it all, I heard the high-pitched wailing of mortally injured *oni*.

Sprinting down the last flight of stairs towards the safe room where Ken and Dad waited, I felt the hot breath of one of the *oni* right behind me. This one had managed to make it past Katsushiro's arrows and was gaining on me. Ahead, Ken was waiting at the door of the safe room, urging me in. I flew past him into the safety of the room.

"Shut the door! Shut the door! Shut the door!"

"Ken, shut the door," my father screamed.

Ken pivoted on one leg and moved to pull the door shut, but he wasn't fast enough for the long arm of the *oni*. He felt the sudden touch of the *oni* on his leg. The huge monster grabbed his ankle and yanked him back hard, its hand clamping down like steel. I was worried his leg might break in its strong grip. He fell on his face as the *oni* pulled him backwards, and his still-sheathed sword clattered out of his hand. I screamed.

"Ken! Ken!"

The hallucinations I had experienced came flooding back to me. Sure that this was to be my brother's final moment, I was nauseated at the thought of his horrible death in the hands of this evil blue monster. All of our efforts were to be for nothing, and worse yet, I was one who had put him in danger. This all happened because I had brought the *oni* into our house. The thought of this evil creature getting Ken made me more angry than afraid.

It was at that moment that I made my decision. Without a second thought, I reached for the sword at my side. My hands were wet with sweat as I sought the hilt. My fingers curled around the diamond-shaped pattern on the handle, and I tugged hard. The sword made a whistling sound as I ripped it from the scabbard. Any hesitation about using the deadly weapon evaporated as I rushed forward to protect my brother.

I saw a look of surprise on my brother's face as I attacked the *oni* with ferocity and speed. Unable to ignore the point of my blade, it reluctantly released Ken to address the new threat. My sword darted in and out, but the *oni* consistently avoided my attack. Each time I swung my *katana*, the blue *oni* ducked or dodged, narrowly escaping before launching a savage counter-attack with its sharp claws. On more than one occasion, I thought I was a goner for sure, but each time I managed to avoid the *oni's* grasp.

'This can't go on forever,' I thought. One false move with those razor-sharp talons and I will be slashed open. I wondered if my armor could withstand it.

Ken scrambled forward and fumbled for his dropped sword, clearly reluctant to use his left leg. At least it didn't look broken. Ignoring the pain, he dropped into a fighting stance and settled in to fight beside me. Our movements were perfectly in sync just as they had been in the Palace when we were practicing. Only now we were using real steel instead of practice blades. I knew what Ken was going to do before he did it, and together we hit the monster with attack after attack.

The *oni* twisted its blue body, desperate to keep away from the lethal edge of our swords, but the closed space of the hallway worked to our advantage. The movement of its massive body was limited by the walls of the hall. Still, the monster was impossibly fast. I flicked my *katana* out and it twisted away. To my left, Ken swung upwards. The blue *oni* shifted its weight and tilted its head back, narrowly saving its chin from my brother's blade.

We repeated this process, each time coming close to our target but not quite able to connect. Then in a flash, I had an inspiration. Changing my strategy, I shot my sword out, deliberately to the left of its head. The monster was standing close to the wall. It dodged my blade, but the wall kept him from moving far. I had effectively pinned him against the wall. This time Ken was there with his blade. The sword went deep into the monster's chest. Ken pushed forward and buried it up to the hilt. It struggled for a moment. Then I heard a gurgling in the back of its throat. It stumbled towards the wall, and I saw a thick blue slime choke up in its mouth.

Flushed with adrenaline I struck the monster with my sword, slashing across its blue neck. The *oni* help up a blue hand, feebly trying to deflect my sword. My blade bit deep. I swung again and again feverishly chopping at the hardened blue skin. I was a wild berserker, hacking the flesh of the monster. Slash slash slash slash. Bits of blue *oni* flesh and slimy blue *oni* blood splattered everywhere.

"Maya! Maya!" Ken yelled at me. I kept going, swinging my blade through the crumpled remains of the *oni*.

When I didn't stop, he tried again, "Okay, Maya. It's okay."

I heard his voice as if from a distance. My hair had slipped out of my ponytail and fell in my eyes with my effort, blocking my vision. I brushed it back and looked up and my brother, startled at my own ferocity. I was drenched in sweat and specks of blue *oni* slime covered me.

"It's okay, Maya. It's dead."

Immediately, Dad was out of the room. He had been watching us.

"Where did you guys learn how to fight like that?" he said in amazement.

"Uh...we took a lesson yesterday," I said, panting. Struggling to catch my breath and recover my composure, I brushed the hair out of my face with my wrist.

"Wow, one whole lesson?" he asked, raising an eyebrow.

"Well, it was a long lesson," Ken said.

"We have to go. They need our help," I said breathlessly, and turned to run back upstairs.

"Maya, no! Wait!" Dad said as Ken and I raced back to where the others were still fighting. The floor was slick with the slime of *oni* blood.

Kyuzo was busy with two *oni*. He moved with lightning quick reflexes, his movements more intuited than planned. His skill with the sword seemed supernatural. Each *oni* attacked with its blue claws, striking with blinding speed at Kyuzo. He expertly blocked, bending his body out of the way and swinging his blade at the throats of his attackers. Despite his skill, he was clearly on the defensive with the two monsters. He had no time to counter-attack, and I worried how long he could avoid the claws of the two monsters. One monster struck. Kyuzo jumped out of the way, blocking.

"Ken, let's get this one," I yelled, pointing my blade at the larger *oni* on the right.

"Just what I was thinking," he said with a grin.

We fell on one of the two hulking blue creatures, attacking it with our *katana*. It pulled away from Kyuzo and turned to face us.

Ken and I were a flurry of sword thrusts. The *oni* snarled at us savagely as it struggled to avoid our blades. This blue *oni* was bigger than the ones I had seen that day and its curled horns were larger too. I guessed that it was older than the others. It also seemed more ferocious. More savage. It snapped and snarled at us as Ken and I fought with it.

"Maya, look at its hand," Ken said between blows.

"What?"

"It has the cut," he said breathlessly. "This is the monster that attacked you in the shrine."

I chanced a quick glance at its hand. Seeing the missing finger and the injury from where it had been wounded in the shrine, I knew immediately this was the same creature that had attacked me before.

In that moment the monster lunged straight at me. Its huge hands with those impossibly sharp talons grabbed me around the waist. Effortlessly, it lifted me up. Just like at the shrine. I shuddered despite myself. I could feel the hate radiating from its monstrous form.

Snarling fiercely, it pulled me closer to its mouth. Its fetid breath clouded the air. I fought an instinct to gag as it brought me closer and closer to its deadly black maw. When my face was inches away, it paused. For a moment, I thought I saw the monster twist up its lips in a savage smile, rows of razor sharp teeth grinning up at me. It was taking some sort of sick pleasure in this. I was more than just a meal to this monster. I could sense its evil delight in my death.

I felt like a trapped animal, but there was nothing I could do to get away. Pain everywhere. All over. My arm, my waist, my chest, my brain. I was a scalding white flash of pain. I struggled to keep from blacking out.

Just as I was about to become a meal for this blue *oni*, Kyuzo caught sight of me.

"Maya!" he yelled. I could barely see him out of the corner of my eye. He turned from his *oni* to my location. He took a step towards me, intending to come and rescue me. In that instant, the *oni* he was fighting picked up a sword that was lying on the ground next to the body of one of its fallen clan members. I had never seen an *oni* use a sword before. The blade was broken and the monster awkwardly held the handle which was tiny in its hand. I watched through a veil of searing pain. Kyuzo's back was turned, and I knew that he didn't see the *oni's* move behind him. I struggled to scream, but the *oni* held me so tightly that I could only croak. Behind Kyuzo the *oni* lunged at him with the broken blade. It drove under Kyuzo's armor and into his chest. The creature lifted Kyuzo up off the ground with the strength of the blow.

I watched in horror as a thin trickle of blood came out of Kyuzo's mouth. His body sagged to the ground dead.

"No!" It was my dad. I was shocked to see he had come out of the den with the little sword that Kyuzo had given him. He leaped into the air, holding the sword like a dagger in both hands. Before the *oni* could turn he landed on the creature's back. The *oni's* back was blue and bumpy and hardened with age.

"Stay...out...of...my...house!" he yelled in short staccato bursts. He stabbed the monster hard and quick, using the sword like an ice pick.

The massive *oni* bucked and snarled, desperately trying to throw him off. It wanted to dislodge him from its back but before it could, Dad sank the sword deep into the *oni's* body. I heard a short crunching sound and saw that the blade was buried up to the hilt in the monster's body. The *oni* screamed and twisted. It was a horrible howling scream, unlike anything I had heard before. Almost human. Certainly not like an animal. The sound iced my blood. The sword anchored Dad to the monster's back. Blue goo bubbled up from where he had stabbed it. It fell and rolled over, trapping my father under its body. The creature was dead, but Dad was stuck.

Meanwhile I struggled with the *oni* that had me in its iron grip. It had one of my hands pinned against my body, but my sword hand was free. Barely conscious, I gripped the handle of my *katana* tightly. It took every ounce of will I had to stay awake. My body throbbed in pain. The monster moved to put my head in its putrid mouth. Its tongue darted out and licked its lips in lascivious anticipation. Its mouth opened wide, and I could see the rows of sharp teeth. Its gaze was fixed on me.

"Not. This. Time." I choked. Using the last of my strength, I drove my sword deep into the monster's mouth. The blade sunk back deep into its throat. My *katana* slowed momentarily when it hit bone but then slid easily into the back of the monster's head. I pulled my hand out quickly, feeling the nick of its sharp teeth on my gauntlet as I did.

The blue *oni* released its grip on my waist, and I slid to the floor, gasping for air. The monster staggered back a step, clutching at the sword stuck in its throat. A look of intense pain crossed its face. It tried unsuccessfully to pull the blade out of its mouth, its massive talons clenching wildly in an attempt to get a grip on the handle of my sword. Both arms fell to its side. Its body went limp. Then it toppled over backwards and died.

"A little help..." Dad said from under the *oni*. He was still pinned under the creature's body. Around me the battle was coming to an end. The samurai were finishing what was left of the *oni*. Heihachi was moving from *oni* to *oni* making sure that each one was dead.

"I count 15 so far," he said, blue goo dripping from his sword.

Ken rolled the blue *oni's* carcass enough for my father to slip out. He put both hands on the monster's shoulder and pushed up, trying to use the strength of his legs. The *oni* was enormous.

"Man, these things really stink," my father said as he extricated himself from under the dead *oni*. He was covered in blue *oni* blood. The room was suddenly quiet. I was stunned, my mind a blank.

The other samurai came into the room. I watched Kanbei clean the blood from his sword and with great care return it to its *saya*.

"Maya, it is over," he said. "We have killed the *oni* and its clan. Your life is free from evil." He spoke slowly.

I looked over to where Kyuzo's body lay motionless on the ground.

"Free from evil..." I repeated almost unable to believe the words I was hearing.

"Kyuzo! No!" It was Katsushiro. He went to where the fallen samurai lay. He pulled up the limp body of his friend and held him in his arms. Kyuzo's head sagged backwards, lifeless.

"Free from evil...but at such a price." I said. I managed to keep from sobbing, but tears filled my eyes. Kyuzo had been an inspiration to all of us. Although the samurai would never speak of it this way, I felt that we had talked Kyuzo into coming with us. He had been reluctant to agree to our plan because he felt the odds were not in our favor. Now he was dead.

Katsushiro knelt beside Kyuzo's body. He choked and I could see that he was crying too. A tear ran down the taut features of his face.

Kanbei's voice was deep, slow and thick with emotion. "Yes, the price was great." He paused, and I thought of Kyuzo's mastery of the sword. He had been such a brave samurai. Kanbei continued to me: "What matters now is what you do with this life. Maya, your life was ransomed at a great price." He looked at me intently.

My heart throbbed in my chest. Finally unable to control myself, hot tears spilled down my cheeks. This time they weren't tears of stress or self-pity, and I didn't try to conceal them. I welcomed these tears, embracing the emotions behind them. I wiped them with the sleeve of my armor, inadvertently smearing blue *oni* blood on my face. I thought of my future and saw a long series of days like the frames of a movie stretched out in front of me. I thought of it as a gift that Kyuzo had given me, a gift that was now mine to use. What would I do with my future?

"I want to be a samurai," I said suddenly. I couldn't believe I was saying this. Would they let me? I stared at Kanbei, not daring to say more. I had hardly been the picture of bravery over the last few days.

"That is not a decision that should be made," Kanbei paused, searching for the right word. "Lightly."

Katsushiro joined us, rubbing his eyes. "The life of a samurai is a difficult one." I could not tell if he was smiling at me.

"And your future is not certain," Heihachi said, coming up behind me. They formed a circle around me now.

I looked at the slain body of Kyuzo on the living room floor. Any doubt that I had in my mind evaporated. I felt a flood of conviction and knew that this was the path for me even if it meant living on the edge of death.

"I want to do it."

Heihachi beamed at me.

"Are you sure?" Kanbei asked.

"I am."

Kanbei looked at my father. Dad nodded.

"And you," Kanbei turned to Heihachi and Katsushiro. "Will you commit to her training? Showing her the way of the samurai in all things?"

"*Hai.* Yes. We will," the samurai said together.

"Well, then..." Kanbei said. "From this day forward you are a samurai, Maya. To be trained in the samurai ways in all things. Welcome. From this day forward, you are our sister in our role to protect people from all evil."

"I commit myself to it with all of my heart," I said my oath solemnly.

The moment was perfect, and as much as I've thought about it, I know I would not change a thing.

There have been times in the years since – with the benefit of time and the clarity that comes with experience – I have wondered what in the world my younger self was thinking. Honestly, I had no idea what I was getting myself into. Sometimes I think it must have been the rush of adrenaline that influenced my decision.  Or Katsushiro.  While I have thought about it frequently, I've never regretted the decision.

It's odd, isn't it?  A terrible experience in my life turned out to be the gateway to my biggest success.  The horrific events of that day in the shrine changed my life forever.  They opened my eyes to a larger world and started me down a path that would change me inside and out.

There is a moment, I believe, when you pass through magic – when the world you know comes to an end.  You return as if waking from a dream.  After that, the world is never the same again.  For me it was that moment in the shrine.

When I said my vows, I worried that I wouldn't be strong enough to follow the way of the samurai.  I remembered all of the times I had cried and all of the times I had been afraid.

Once, not long after that, I confessed to Kanbei how scared I had been.

"I never thought that you would not be afraid," he told me. "I just trusted you to never give up."

That was many years ago, but I remember it as if it happened yesterday.  In time and with great effort, my samurai skills improved.  Of course, I never could have done it alone.  It was the courage and the sacrifice of the samurai that inspired me.  Gradually, the vague outline of Maya the Girl slowly filled out into Maya the Samurai.

You know, I've learned since then something about the making of a samurai sword.  The steel of the blade is made in a furnace using iron and carbon.   When these two are heated together, something amazing happens.  A complex change occurs, fusing the iron and carbon together.  All of it happens on the atomic level.  The carbon makes the steel strong, while the iron makes the steel tough.  You want a blade that can take a lot.  A tough metal doesn't break – it bends.

At some point, I realized the attack by the blue *oni* was my furnace.  I changed in the process.  One moment in the shrine on that December day changed the course of my life forever.  What would have happened if I had never left the house?  If I had stayed at the breakfast table instead of leaving with Ken?  If I had gone through the *torii* instead of around?  I'll never know, but I do know that the experience changed the kind of person I am.  I see that I became stronger in a way I never would have believed possible.

Every human needs to know what they are fighting for. That's what the woman in the white *kimono* had told me. My time in the shrine had changed me. I realized I was fighting for a much larger world – just a world most people never see.

Of course, I didn't know it then, but my adventures had only just begun.

## Epilogue

A fter the battle, we cleaned the house for several hours. The samurai were as efficient and diligent at clean up as they were at fighting. I felt a new sense of camaraderie with the samurai now that I was one of them. We shared a sense of victory over evil and the feeling of combined purpose.

Just before noon Kanbei called for a truck that came to pick up the bodies of the slain *oni*.

"It wouldn't do to have rotting *oni* corpses lying in the street," he said matter-of-factly.

Soon after, a blue garbage truck arrived. It looked like every garbage truck I had ever seen in Japan, but I suspected its crew must be affiliated with Kanbei. I stared at the truck for a moment and tried to relax my eyes. Katsushiro had taught me to use soft eyes (his words). According to him, soft eyes allowed one to see the truth of an object and not be thwarted by the blindness. I let me eyes relax and tried to let my preconceptions fade. Nothing. It was still just a blue garbage truck. The crew jumped out and began to load the slaughtered monsters onto the truck. I was about to turn away when I noticed that all of the garbage collectors had pony tails. Before they left I peeked in the cab of the truck and spotted a samurai sword sitting on a rack behind the driver's seat. I gave my best bow as they drove away.

We cleaned the house methodically, but I got the feeling that it was never going to smell the same. The stench of *oni* permeated every room.

"This is what 'victory' smells like," Heihachi told me.

Meanwhile, my body was cleaning the *oni* toxins out of my system. To this day I'm not sure how that worked. Perhaps it was the death of the *oni* that had licked me. That seems the most likely explanation. But sometimes I wonder if it was not the process of facing my fears. Maybe picking up that *katana* and attacking that *oni* caused some change in me. In any event, my mind cleared and I began to feel like myself again.

I thought about how my life would be from now on. My father had given me permission to complete my samurai training, but he made me promise to finish school. It wasn't easy to convince him given what he knew about the samurai. I think he figured I was going to do it anyway and he may as well give me his blessing. I was glad for his support. I wondered what it would be like to return to school now that I was a samurai.

"Am I sworn to secrecy?" I asked Kanbei very seriously.

"Why would that be required?" he seemed surprised.

"I don't know. I just thought…"

"Maya, you've met a great evil and have overcome. That is a story I'd want you to share with people, not keep a secret. But remember, not everyone will be able to accept it."

"Hey, didn't you have something at school today?" Dad asked out of the blue.

"Oh no! The Winter Jam!" I had forgotten all about it in the excitement of everything that had happened.

I looked at Kanbei. I didn't know if I should ask him. I desperately wanted to get to my school.

He read my expression and knew what I was thinking. Without speaking to me directly, he brought the others together. They conferred briefly in Japanese.

Switching to English for my benefit, he said, "Gentlemen, our newest samurai needs to get to her school. Shall we help her?"

"Yes, sir!" came the immediate response. We went out to the motorcycles which were undisturbed in the parking lot. In just a few minutes we were flying on the expressway out to school. I sat with Heihachi again. Ken was with Katsushiro and my father rode on Kyuzo's bike. We reached the school in twenty minutes.

161

"There you are, Maya," said Mr. B as we walked onto campus. "You are on in five minutes. I have been looking all over for you."

Glancing up from his clipboard, he caught sight of the three samurai with us.

"Good, you guys are already in costume. Now go back stage and wait for your names to be called."

We walked away towards the back-stage area to prepare for our performance.

"He could see our samurai clothes?" I asked Kanbei when I thought we were out of earshot.

"Yes, that is curious," Kanbei laughed good-naturedly. "Perhaps it is close to what he was expecting."

As we walked away Mr. B called to us, "Hey, by the way, what is the name of your group?"

Without missing a beat Kanbei called back, "We are the Samurai."

Mr. B wrote it down on his clipboard.

When our time came, we all walked out on stage together.

## ABOUT THE AUTHOR

David Keuning studied Japanese language and literature at Yale University. He lives in Honolulu with his wife, his two children and his faithful dog Hanako. This is his first novel.